ROMANSGROVE

ROMANSGROVE

Mabel Esther Allan

ILLUSTRATED BY
GAIL OWENS

Atheneum 1975 *New York*

Library of Congress
Cataloging in Publication Data

Allan, Mabel Esther.   Romansgrove.
Summary: Exploring their new country home,
Claire and Richard suddenly find themselves seventy
years in the past, a visit that changes the course
of many lives, including their own.
[1. Space and time—Fiction] I. Owens, Gail.
II. Title.   PZ7.A4Rr   [Fic]   75-9628
ISBN 0-689-30471-4

Published simultaneously in Canada by
McClelland & Stewart, Ltd.
Manufactured in the United States of America
Printed by Sentry Press, New York
Bound by The Book Press
Brattleboro, Vermont
First Edition

CONTENTS

ROMANSGROVE

I

THE SUMMER
WOODS

"I'm going to listen," said Clare, tight-lipped.

"You can't. It wouldn't be . . ."

"Oh, don't start that, Rich!" Clare retorted furiously. "This is no time for saying 'It wouldn't be honest!' I don't see what honesty has to do with it. We shall hear all about it soon, anyway. I hope so, at least."

"Then . . ."

"I have to know *now*. I can't wait. I'll tell Dad I listened. I can't stand any more!" Clare's voice began to shake.

Richard stared at her. He was almost thirteen, just a year younger than Clare, and the two had always been close. Now he suddenly realized that Clare was near the breaking point. Come to that, he wasn't far off it himself. The troubles and tensions within the family had gone on too long. If something didn't happen soon—some hopeful, constructive thing—there would be an emotional explosion.

Clare stared back from the top of the stairs. She was thin and brown haired, with a pale, tense face. Her eyes looked enormous, and her lips were still tight. Her cheekbones stood out, and Richard thought suddenly, with a feeling of shock: "She looks more like forty than not quite fourteen."

"Oh, go on, then," he said. "I'll come, too. We won't have to go very near. They haven't quite shut the door."

They went down the narrow stairs, one behind the other. It was a small Victorian house, a very lived-in house, the furniture and carpets a little shabby. But there were pictures and even flowers . . . a big arrangement of red roses from the back garden on the table in the hall. Their smell made Clare feel sick, and everything seemed clearer than usual; she found herself noticing each worn patch on the hall carpet, dust on an old carved chair. Their mother had bothered with flowers, but had not polished with her former energy. Not even when she knew that Mr. Drake was coming.

"We are all past caring about most of the little things," Clare said to herself.

The trouble had started six months earlier, at the end of January, when Mr. Manley had had a serious operation. He was an accountant, and he worked for a big firm on the outskirts of the city where they lived. He had expected to be off work for around two months, but he had not made the good recovery that had been foretold. It had been four months before he had returned to work, and by then he was a changed man. Irritable, easily tired, finding his old way of life an almost impossible effort.

Their pleasant, safe family life now seemed a far dream to Clare and Richard, and probably to their mother also. Though she had never once discussed the real depths of the matter with them. In a way that was the very worst of the trouble.

"Your father needs a change of scene. A different kind of life," was the most she had allowed herself to say. Then on another occasion, only a few days ago: "The doctor says there's nothing radically wrong with him now, but he shouldn't have gone back to Wells and Bane. Yet he's forty-two. It isn't easy, these days, for a man of that age to find the right kind of job, even though he's a chartered accountant." Then she had left them abruptly, obviously not wanting to discuss the matter.

Forty-two seemed old, in a way, but people lived to be ninety. And then, on this Saturday morning, Mr. Drake, one of the directors of Wells and Bane, had telephoned to ask if he might come to see them. He had a suggestion to make about a new job, he had said.

Mr. Drake arrived promptly at three o'clock, and it was barely five minutes later as Clare and Richard crept along the hall. The clock on the wall by the kitchen door ticked loudly, like someone's heart.

They couldn't have missed very much, Clare decided.

"And I *will* tell Dad I listened," she said to herself. Even though he'd probably be angry, she knew, or sarcastic in the way she hated. He never used to speak to them like that. He'd always had his bitter side, but about life . . . never directed at them. Mother had always said it was his hard boyhood that made him like that. But he had always been gentle to them.

Mr. Drake had a loud, confident North Country voice. He was evidently finishing a long speech.

"So I thought, Bill—" they had known him for years, and had even visited his house on several occasions—"that it would be just the thing for you. Country air, and a wonderful part of the Cotswolds. Hills and woods, and the kids could go to school in the nearest town, Painsden. It would all be so much easier for you, and that's what the doctor ordered, isn't it? No driving to and from work in the rush hour, and South Lodge is a charming house. I've seen it. Been there once or twice to visit with the Romans. My mother came from those parts. Once you've seen Romansgrove you'll be hooked. It's quite a place. And as estate accountant . . ."

Romansgrove. Clare was standing so tensely that she ached all over, but the word cut into her mind with strange force. Romansgrove! She met her brother's eyes. Richard nodded slightly, as if agreeing that his interest was caught, too. Richard cared about the past, whether it concerned the Second World War, the Stuarts or the Tudors, or even the Roman occupation of Britain nearly two thousand years ago.

"The job's yours, if you want it," Mr. Drake declared, in loud triumph. "You'll have to go down for an

interview, but just say the word, and I'm sure it'll be
fixed. I telephoned Alan Roman this morning as soon as
I saw the advertisement in *The Times*. He's the second
Lord Romansgrove; his father was given the title for his
services to agriculture."

So far their father hadn't had a chance to say a word,
and he didn't speak now. It was their mother who said,
in a very controlled voice:

"It's very good of you to think of us . . . to do this
for Bill. I'm sure it would be the very thing, if—"

Clare and Richard had moved close together, Clare
gripping Richard's hand. The clock ticked loudly, stab-
bing the silence. Clare could imagine just how they
looked inside; her father, tall and thin, his gray-brown
hair a little rumpled, sitting on the edge of a chair, and
her mother frowning anxiously, her hands clenched in
the way they had so often been lately.

Then Mr. Manley spoke. His voice sounded harsh,
though its tone was usually well modulated.

"Yes, it *is* good of you. I'm grateful. But I can't go to
Romansgrove. I disapprove of great estates . . . land-
owners. Oh, I've no doubt that this Lord Romansgrove
pays his workers better than my father was paid, and my
grandfather. He has to; things are different now. But I
have never been able to forget the way we lived. My
father, and his father, worked for a big farmer in
Cheshire. They were unskilled farm workers, and my
dad was paid thirty shillings a week, and no overtime, as
recently as the early 1940s. *Thirty* shillings, and he sometimes worked from 6:00 in the morning until 10:00 at
night. In summer, when it was harvesttime. There *should*

have been overtime, but that farmer hardly ever paid them a penny extra. Sometimes my dad had to go and *ask* for his wages. It was just that the old devil liked to torture folk . . ."

"Yes, but . . ."

"We had a free cottage, and we kept hens and grew some vegetables, but my father had a bent back at thirty from carrying heavy sacks, and my mother looked fifty when she couldn't have been much over thirty. When I was around nine, I remember noticing for the first time how worn her face was. She was born in poverty, and she was poor all her life. Our cottage was three hundred years old, and the kitchen had an earth floor. There was no water indoors . . . just a faucet in the yard. And no proper sanitation. We had to go to a terrible little place outdoors, even when the snow was on the ground."

"Yes, but, Bill lad . . ." Mr. Drake was sixty-five, but even so it sounded strange to hear their father spoken to as if he were a boy.

Clare took a harder grip on Richard's hand and turned her white face to his, making a desperate grimace. *Nothing* would stop their father when he was well launched on the subject of his boyhood. They had heard it endlessly. And he wouldn't go to Romansgrove, even though it was in the Cotswolds, and there were trees and hills, and a good job waiting. Estate accountant. It sounded fine.

"My parents died before their time. Died in poverty and discomfort. And I got away. I was clever, and I studied and managed somehow until I was qualified. Figures were always my thing. I don't know where the children get their imaginations. But you can see I can't go back, especially to dealing with farm workers' wages."

"It wouldn't only be that. It's a vast estate. Now you just listen to me," said Mr. Drake forcefully. "I know you're something of a Socialist . . ."

"Not 'something.' "

"Well, I know you did good work on the City Council for several years, until ill health made you give it up. Lord Romansgrove isn't the kind of man you fear and despise. He lives in a big house, it's true, but it's turned into flats, and he works as hard as any of his employees. Mean to say you've never heard of Romansgrove?"

"No, I don't think so." Mr. Manley sounded tired suddenly, and only slightly irritable.

"It's tops for working conditions. All the old cottages have been modernized, and many new houses built. The workers are paid the highest rates, and, apart from that, they take bonuses out of the estate. If there's a good year, everyone benefits. It's the best run place in England, and it made agricultural history a generation or two ago. The South Lodge is a good small house. Quite modern. Romansgrove House was only built this century."

"I thought you said, when you started, that the Roman family were supposed to have been there since the Dark Ages. Really since the Roman occupation of Britain." Clare relaxed slightly. Her father sounded different; interested.

"Well, that's the legend, I suppose, because of the

surname. There was another house, of course. I don't know the story. People often pull down old houses and build new ones on the site. You know very plain, Bill," Mr. Drake's voice changed, "that if you stay here you'll crack up good and proper. And you owe it to that son and daughter of yours to make a change and pull yourself together. I saw them waiting at the bus stop by their school last week. Clare looks awful, as if a strong wind would snap her, and the boy isn't much better. Alice, you're a sensible woman. Schoolteachers must have brains..."

"I'm not teaching now," said Mrs. Manley. "I gave it up when Bill had his operation."

"I know that. You could take it up again, I suppose. Apply to Painsden; part-time or something. But you talk sense to your husband here. See he gets his application into the mail. Here's the advertisement. I cut it out of The *Times*. And I'll have another word with Alan Roman. It's your place; I feel that in my bones. It'll wipe out all that stuff about earth floors and closets down the garden. My own dad started life in a moorland cottage and went to work in a cotton mill at twelve. I sympathize."

"I'll get some tea." Mrs. Manley sounded different, as if much of her tension was gone.

"No tea, thank you. I must be off. Use your loaf, Bill, as we say in the North. That clever head of yours. Get cracking."

There were movements within the room, and Clare and Richard raced to the top of the stairs before the door opened to its fullest. Voices sounded in the hall, but by then they were in Richard's room, with the door shut. Clare lay flat on his bed, her thin arms behind her head, her feet kicking rhythmically in a kind of triumph.

"I think he'll go, Rich. I think we'll all go to Romansgrove. It sounds a fabulous place, and . . . maybe things will be better."

"Are you going to tell them we listened?" Richard asked. He stood by the window, staring out at the summer garden and the backs of the houses opposite. The light was thick and golden, the sky a hazy, luminous blue.

"I don't know. Later, I think. I daren't upset Dad now. Just let him get that letter written and into the mail. I can't bear it if it falls through now."

The letter was mailed, and they were told. Then Clare, relaxed by the changed atmosphere, did confess to their listening. It was taken as natural.

"You'd have heard Drake's voice at the top of the stairs," their father said. "Needn't have come down. Well, he may be right. Romansgrove may be special. But that South Lodge . . . we're not going to be gate-keepers."

"Open the gate and curtsy as her ladyship goes past," said Clare, and then was horrified by her own tactlessness.

She had a vision of herself holding a great iron gate and a handsome woman in a bonnet smiling at her from a carriage. It was a silly thought, she told herself, blinking nervously at her father. A Rolls, probably, and Lady Romansgrove wearing the latest Paris creation. Or was that silly, too? She might be wearing slacks and a sweater and riding a bicycle. Or a horse, of course.

There was no comment to her remark, but her father's face tightened momentarily.

It all happened very quickly, which was an enormous relief. Lord Romansgrove received the application on Monday morning, and telephoned at once to ask Mr. Manley if he could come down Wednesday. Mr. Drake was delighted, and time off from Wells and Bane was easily arranged. When Clare and Richard left for school on Wednesday, their father had already driven away, heading for the motorway that led south.

He telephoned that evening to say he had agreed to take the job and would be home by lunchtime the next day. So Mrs. Manley, Clare and Richard had a celebration supper and were almost hysterically gay. Mrs. Manley talked more seriously before they went to bed, however.

"Look, I'm sorry. I *couldn't* talk about it. I felt awful, too, all these months. But I do believe things will improve now, and we'll get back to normal, or better than normal. I hope you don't mind leaving your school. We'll have to arrange a transfer to a school in Painsden. Everything will be new, but you'll be free until September. Of course we don't know how soon we'll go. We'll have to sell this house, but there shouldn't be any difficulty over that."

Clare and Richard exchanged glances. School had become entangled with their home troubles, and they hadn't done so well lately. They had begun to lose touch with their friends, too. Adversity had drawn them together and away from outside contacts. Leaving was no problem.

"We don't mind a bit, Mother," said Clare. "Romansgrove . . . Romansgrove. Real deep country in summer. I suppose not at all like the Northern moors and hills?"

"Not like them at all," she agreed, smiling. "I used to know the Cotswold country when I was young, though not that particular part. Villages where all the houses are built of golden stone, with lovely tiled roofs, and the earth is a kind of ocher shade . . . tawny gold."

On Thursday they didn't see their father until 4:30, when they returned together from school. He looked tired but relaxed, and though he'd already told his story once, he told it again.

"I met Lord Romansgrove at the estate office in the village. He really seems very nice. I told him about my politics, and just a little about my early life in Cheshire, and he said he thought I'd approve of Romansgrove. And if I had any ideas I could tell him. No, I didn't go to the big house, but I could see it on the hillside. Very large and plain. Brick, I think, not built of the local stone. He drove me around a little, and I saw South Farm and East Farm, and of course South Lodge. It's a splendid house, just big enough, and with everything modern. You'll approve of it, Alice, I'm sure." He caught Clare's glance and laughed, so that the lines didn't show for a moment on his face. "The gates are operated by electricity from the house, but are usually open in the daytime. There's a telephone for late visitors, and a little gate in the big one. There'll be no curtsying."

"I never really thought . . ." Clare mumbled.

"He wants me to start as soon as possible, and Drake

has said they'll release me as soon as they've found some-one to take my place. By the end of July, if we can sell the house . . . It'll mean a lot of quick work."

The house was sold almost as soon as it was adver-tised, and the sale went through with miraculous speed. Clare and Richard finished school on July 20, and by then there was only some sorting of possessions to be done, and packing. Mr. Manley still had his sharp, irri-table times, and there were two terrible days when he was convinced he had done the wrong thing.

"My principles should have stopped me from working for a landowner . . . a *lord*," he said, and Clare felt sick again. She lay on the hot, dry grass in the garden, trying to read and not taking in a word.

"But he can't change his mind now," Richard said, sitting down beside her. "We'll have to go to Romans-grove. This house is sold, and the job's all fixed. Don't worry. His mood will pass."

Mr. Manley's black mood did pass, and the last tasks were finished. They left on Wednesday, July 31, with the furniture following in a huge truck. It was a thun-dery day, with bursts of hot sunshine, and the motorway was crowded with traffic. But at last they left it and were on ordinary roads, heading into country that grew richer with every mile. There were fields of ripening barley, oats and wheat on either side, and eventually they extended up the slopes of rounded hills. There were wild flowers by the wayside, and the trees were heavy with summer growth. Sweet, hot smells blew in through the open windows. Finally there was a signpost that said: ROMANSGROVE, 2 MILES.

"We're approaching the valley from the south," Mr. Manley explained. "The direct road from the North is over the hills and very narrow and winding."

Clare and Richard were hot and restless, but the signpost filled them with a strong excitement. They drove into a wide valley, very lush and obviously productive. A stormy wind rippled through fields of silver barley and tall, stiff wheat nearly ready for harvesting. In pasture fields were herds of cows.

Romansgrove village dreamed around a very clean duck pond. The cottages were built of golden stone and covered with creepers and yellow roses. There was a smooth green, an ancient church with a tower, an Elizabethan vicarage, a little store and a post office. Also a very ancient inn.

"This is the old part," said Mr. Manley. "But all the cottages have been modernized, with bathrooms built on at the back. Now this is the other part. Newer houses for estate workers, and that big building is where most of the social activities take place. There's the estate office."

But Clare and Richard had eyes only for the wider scene. There, on the eastern slope of the valley, was the big house their father had described after his visit; not old, not romantic, but impressive. On the other side of the valley was an enormously thick belt of woodland, almost a forest, seeming to extend for miles. It looked dark and secret in the shifting gold of late afternoon.

"That," said Mr. Manley, "is Roman's Grove. And here we are at the south entrance to Romansgrove House. This is South Lodge, our new home."

2

THE
PENDANT

The lodge was just beyond the great open gates, on the right-hand side, and the driveway that led to the big house almost immediately curved on between laurel and rhododendron bushes and disappeared.

Mr. Manley stopped the car behind the lodge, in a small, partly fenced yard, and Clare and Richard scrambled out. Without a word to each other, but moving as one, they walked back the way they had come until they were outside the gates. They stood there, stretching their limbs in the hot sun, breathing deeply. The air was thick with fragrance . . . scents of warm grass and flowers.

"Breathe deeply!" said Clare. "The moors smelled

good, but this is real summer."

The open gates were high and made of a complicated pattern in ironwork, each with a gold-painted center. The two high gateposts were topped by stone heads.

"Romans, do you think?" asked Richard. "They seem to be wearing helmets."

On the left-hand post was the word ROMANSGROVE, and on the right HOUSE.

South Lodge was built of uncompromising, fairly modern brick, but was half smothered in yellow roses, which softened its practical lines. A white-painted front door was a few yards inside the gates, and there was a small garden that someone had kept in order.

"I wish it were old," said Clare, "and built of that lovely golden stone like the ones in the village. I wonder why they rebuilt the lodge when they were rebuilding the big house?"

"They were thinking of the workers," her brother said. "A bathroom, you know, and all the rest of it."

"But they could have modernized it the way they did the cottages in the village." She turned slowly and crossed the narrow road to a field gate. Beside the gate there was a stile, with a footpath sign, and beyond, a path went straight across a field of oats, ripe for harvesting. Among the golden oats were scarlet poppies and a few cornflowers of a vivid royal blue, but it was the grass-grown path that held Clare's attention. She leaned her chin on the top of the five-barred gate and stared.

"See how it goes? There's another stile at the far side of the field. I believe this path leads straight across the valley to Roman's Grove."

Richard leaned beside her, gazing across the valley, then upward to the brooding trees.

"I wonder how soon we can go?" he mused. "We'll have to help."

"Tomorrow, perhaps. There's something curious about it. I want to go but I feel scared of it, too. I never was in a forest. Neither were you, Rich. I wonder if the ancient Romans haunt it?"

"No, though they do say you can still find a certain kind of white snail the Romans liked," said a voice behind them, and they both jumped and spun around.

They had not heard him approach. He looked to be about their father's age and was deeply suntanned. He wore very old trousers and an open-necked shirt; a handsome man, with very blue, intelligent eyes.

One of the estate workers? But his voice . . .

"You'll be the Manley children?" he said. "Clare and Richard, I believe. I had an aunt called Clare, and we very nearly gave the name to our daughter. I'm Alan Roman. Have you been here long? I meant to be here to welcome you."

Lord Romansgrove . . . What about that curtsy? Clare asked herself, with amusement and doubt. *Did* one? No, of course not . . . absurd. Her father would have a fit if he knew she kept on thinking in such an archaic way. In his view Lord Romansgrove was a perfectly ordinary man, with no right to own a huge piece of inherited property.

Come to that he did look ordinary, even shabby. And he had said: "I'm Alan Roman." Not: "I am the second Lord Romansgrove, owner of all this."

"Only about five minutes, Sir," Richard explained. "We got out of the car and came to look. It's . . . we're used to the Northern moors. We've never seen country like this; so rich and with so many trees. Roman's Grove . . . are there really white snails?"

"There are said to be, though I've roamed the Grove all my life and never seen one. There are traces of a Roman villa, but not of much interest in a countryside where there are one or two superb examples. I have found Roman coins and once a bit of green Roman glass. Interested in archaeology?"

"Oh, yes." Richard's face was flushed with heat and eagerness. "Any kind of history."

"So is my daughter Victoria. She's away just now. She went to stay with an aunt when school finished, but she'll be home soon. I'd better go and speak to your parents. My wife will be down later. Oh, there comes your furniture!"

The big truck came cautiously along the narrow road and stopped. Lord Romansgrove hurried forward to speak to the driver and his companion, and Clare and Richard turned back to the green path through the oats that led to the distant dark mass of trees.

"I can see that we've missed something, not growing up in the country," said Richard.

"Well, we're going to grow up in it now, and Father wouldn't agree with you. Not *his* kind of country childhood, all poverty, and going to a little country school that had hardly any *books*."

"I know. And, we've had other things. A good public library, and being taken to concerts and a good art gallery." Richard picked a long blade of grass and chewed it absently. "Maybe we'll miss them. And there's winter, of course. How will it be then?"

"Beautiful," said Clare, with her chin on the gate again. "The leaves will fall in Roman's Grove, and then we'll see the real shapes of the trees. And this country will be even more secret and strange in the cold and dark."

"Mud and rain and long dark evenings . . . Oh, all right, I don't suppose we'll mind. There's a lot to learn here. I want to see it all."

It was three hours later before there was any real semblance of order. Clare and Richard had helped where they could, and everyone had grown hot and dirty. But a break for tea helped to revive energy, and by seven o'clock, when the thunder clouds were heavy overhead, the worst was over. Clare stood in her tiny bedroom that looked straight across the valley to Roman's Grove and could already see that the house might soon be "home."

When she went down the narrow flight of stairs, there was a stranger in the kitchen; a tall, suntanned woman, wearing slacks and an old pink blouse. She had fair hair and was very slim. She was busy taking things out of a plastic shopping bag.

"You see, I know what it's like. I expect you brought some food with you, but, just in case you didn't, I knew the store and the butcher's would be closed this afternoon . . . early closing. So here are some lamb cutlets, and frozen fish, if you'd sooner have that. A fresh loaf, and peas just picked, and raspberries."

"It's very good of you," Mrs. Manley said, and turned to see Clare and Richard. "These are my son and daughter. Richard is nearly thirteen and Clare will soon be fourteen. Children, this is Lady Romansgrove, and she ..."

A sudden clap of thunder startled them all. Lady Romansgrove said: "Hello, you two!" And then, hastily: "I'd better fly, or I'll get soaked. See you all tomorrow!" And she ran out through the open door, mounted a bicycle that needed cleaning, and peddled out of the yard and away up the driveway.

Clare leaned against the table, giggling helplessly. So it was slacks and a bicycle ... not a horse, and certainly not a Rolls, though the Romans would probably own a big car. A carriage and pair was very far in the past.

How nice they both seemed. Would Victoria be the same? She probably went to a boarding school and had friends of her own. *Their* friends would be the children of other estate workers.

With lightning flashing, and the heavy summer rain pouring down, Mrs. Manley hastily cooked the meal. Clare wandered to the living room window. Roman's Grove was almost lost in the rainy gloom, but sweet fragrances came in through the partly opened window. The rain was falling so straight and hard that not a drop came in.

It seemed incredible that only twelve hours earlier they had been in the North. Now, across the valley, a great wood brooded and waited to be explored.

It was nearly two o'clock the next afternoon before the chance to explore came. Their father had gone off soon after 8:30 to start work, and he had said he might be busy getting settled, so he would not come home for lunch. The inn might provide a quick meal, or at any rate sandwiches. He did not seem to be dreading the new experience, and walked away briskly through the great gates, so the atmosphere was cheerful.

Clare and Richard were kept busy all morning emptying boxes and cartons, and arranging some of their own possessions. Mrs. Manley walked to the village to investigate the butcher's and the general store, and came back laden.

"Everyone seems very friendly," she said. "The store is quite well stocked, and the butcher's is up a little side lane. The post office is in one of the prettiest cottages; did you notice yesterday? The inn is called the Roman Arms, and it does do snacks and lunches, so your father will be all right. There's not much else, except that big village hall. There seems to be plenty going on there. I stopped to look at the notices. Bingo, whist drives, dances. I passed the estate office, of course, but I didn't go in. I thought it was better to leave your father to get settled."

"Isn't there a school?" asked Clare.

"Oh, yes. A school and a schoolhouse, but the school is only for young children. All the older ones go to Painsden in a school bus, as you will. Well, have you finished? Oh, it looks fairly tidy now. Let's have lunch."

So they had lunch, and helped to wash the dishes, and then, at last, they were free. Free to climb the stile and set off along the narrow path through the golden oats. Clare picked two poppies, put them behind her ears and turned her face toward the far trees.

"Roman's Grove, here we come. Richard, in a kind of way I'm still scared. It looks so permanent. As if it's been there for centuries waiting to swallow us up."

"It's just a wood," her brother said, though underneath he had the same feeling. In that vast wood, nearly two thousand years before, the Romans had lived; not the family, but men who had once come from Rome. "I want to find the traces of a villa and look for coins. I wish *I* could find some Roman glass. Do you remember that Roman glass we saw in the museum? Bottles in different shapes, all greenish?"

The Romans seemed to Clare incredibly remote, but the weight of history certainly lay over the valley. The Roman family might not have started nearly two thousand years ago, but they had been there a very long time, through several centuries, at least. And the village had been there, and ordinary people living in other times.

Almost in silence they crossed the second field, walking through the silky pale-gold barley by way of the continuing green path. The storm had not cooled the air. It was hotter than ever, and everywhere was deliciously steamy as well as a little soggy underfoot. Clare breathed deeply of the summer sweetness, and absently brushed away flies.

Then they crossed a narrow, rutted lane, and took to the path again. Without doubt it was going straight to Roman's Grove, and, after several more fields, it began climbing steadily. The vastness of the Grove loomed over them, dark green and absolutely silent in the breathless afternoon. In the last sloping field the sun was still beating down on their heads and bare arms, and they paused to look back at the big house on the opposite slope, and their own new home, looking very small and unimportant.

Turning slightly, they could see some of the new estate houses down the valley, and the tower of the church rising among trees. Between the end of the Roman's Grove ridge and the village was a farm . . . a big cluster of buildings.

"That must be South Farm," said Richard. "We can't see East Farm; its behind the village somewhere over there. I remember Father mentioning it. But look!" He turned Clare until they were looking up the valley, where the land gradually rose to another ridge. "More farm buildings. North Farm, I suppose. We'd get to it if we went on up the road past South Lodge."

"I don't know how you know which is North and South," said Clare, staring at the pattern of green and golden fields, slightly dimmed by the heat haze.

"I do, anyway. I'm going to make a map, when I know it a little better." He added thoughtfully: "Whoever planned Romansgrove House, and all the other newer ones, wasn't thinking about beauty and trying to fit them into the landscape."

They turned again toward Roman's Grove, walking slowly, a trifle reluctant to be absorbed into the green gloom. At close hand it lost none of its somber power. A last stile took them into the wood, and then the trees enveloped them. Trees . . . An outer rim of holly, dark, shiny-leaved and oppressive, and then . . .

"What kind of trees?" asked Clare, looking upward and tripping over a root.

Richard didn't know much about trees, but he could see that they were not all the same. Oaks, he knew, and the tall ones with smooth gray trunks must be beech.

"Mixed woodland," he remarked. "That's what I think you call it. Oak and beech and those might be sweet chestnut. They all look very old. I thought estates sold timber. Perhaps the Romans don't touch Roman's Grove."

The path, which had been clear enough over the fields, though some of the stiles had been overgrown with nettles, suddenly became so deep in bracken and brambles it was obvious that few people came into Roman's Grove. The path in the valley might have been an ancient right of way, and there was no sign of any kind to say that the wood was private. But if tourists and walkers came this way, they certainly didn't venture into what Clare still thought of as "the forest."

The two pushed and struggled and made detours. Luckily both were wearing jeans, for otherwise their legs would have been torn to pieces. As it was their bare arms soon bore many scratches. It was hot in Roman's Grove, though the sunlight came only in occasional small patterns of golden light. In the main they were moving through a green, eerie world, awesome in its absolute solitude.

Then, tired and secretly afraid they would never find their way out of the wood, they reached a more definite path, extending to their left and right. Their sandaled feet stamped on bare earth for a short while after they turned right, and, even when bracken encroached again, there were still clear patches. Feeling more comfortable, Richard began to search on either side, scuffing his feet through old fallen leaves, lifting occasional stones. He found no Roman coins or pieces of green glass, but quite by chance stumbled on the traces of the Roman villa.

His shout of triumph brought Clare plunging after him, and there it was, all that was left of that lost civilization. A few low walls, with a scattering of small Roman bricks in the undergrowth, and a tumbledown wooden shed over a damaged stretch of mosaic pavement. Falling on their knees within the structure, they could see a dim picture in the center of the black and white tiles. The colors were faded, but they could make out a design that looked like a lion, and, a few feet away, a man's head.

Clare sat back on her heels and tried to imagine what it must have been like. They had learned about it in school. How the Romans lived in a very comfortable way . . . the rich ones. Central heating, even. But it was too far back, too utterly remote. She shivered even while the sweat lay on her forehead.

"Let's go on," she said.

They returned to the path, which continued on through the wood, as if it might run forever. Once it plunged down into a hollow, and Clare, dreaming, didn't notice a long, curving root. She fell headlong, nearly striking her face against an ancient tree trunk. Her shriek echoed through the trees, and Richard rushed to help her to her feet.

"Did you hurt yourself?" he asked.

Clare brushed her earthy hands together, and shook her head.

"No-o. I don't think so. I was just surprised."

"Come on, then."

But Clare stood unmoving by the tree. The wood had grown completely silent. There was not the faintest rustle of leaves, not a single bird song. Richard glanced at her face and felt uneasy.

"What's the matter? Sure you didn't bang your head?"

Clare said nothing but sank slowly to her knees and put her right hand into a hole between the roots. She brought it out filled with old leaves.

"Here's something else," she said, scattering the leaves and revealing a small object. "I've found you something Roman, Rich. Look at it!"

The thing was covered with earth. Richard wiped it with his hand and blew on it. Clare offered him a paper handkerchief, and after several rubs it began to take on shape, though it was still very dirty. It was made of dull metal and was round, about two inches across. The metal was wrought into a pattern of leaves or flowers. A short piece of fine chain dangled from the top.

"A sort of medallion," said Clare.

"I don't think it's Roman," her brother remarked. "The workmanship seems much too delicate. I should think it's fairly modern. A pendant, I suppose. It's lain hidden here for some time, but it might clean up a bit more. Try silver polish when we get home." Then he glanced at Clare; she looked quite normal now. "But how did you know it was there, Clare?"

"I didn't. I just found it," she said, looking surprised.

"But you *must* have known. You knelt down and put your hand quite deliberately into that hole. And your arm went in half way to your elbow. You couldn't possibly have seen the pendant when you fell. It was all among the leaves, anyway."

"Well, I did find it," she said, a little impatiently. "I guess I felt something when I fell. So don't make a mystery of it, Rich. This place is spooky enough. Give it to me."

Clare took the pendant and dropped it into the pocket in her old green blouse. The pendant lay small and hard against her heart as they went on, going slowly now, wondering how much farther it would be to the end of the wood. They didn't speak, but each knew that the other wanted to turn back . . . well, half wanted to. Yet something pulled them both on, an urge to explore. It was strange, Clare thought, how close she and Richard had grown lately, so that they didn't even need to talk. As young children they had often been taken for twins, for there was barely a year between them and Richard had been tall for his age. *Then* they had been inseparable, but, of course, later they had made other friends and grown a little apart. The family troubles and the long months of near nightmare had brought them together again. It was the one good thing that had come out of adversity. That, and maybe Romansgrove.

Her mind busy, she pushed her way through the last tangle of undergrowth, heading into golden light. This was the end of the wood at last. And . . . she took a few steps forward, out of the trees, then stopped, blinking and staring in amazement and delight. For the scene that confronted her was a complete surprise.

There was a big stretch of grass, short and smooth, with a lake in a gentle hollow, then shallow terraces, edged with low stone balustrades, rising to a great house. It was built of the golden local stone, with an old tiled roof and twisted Tudor chimneys. It stood there, dominating the rise, beautiful and old. She saw the stone-mullioned windows catching the light and smelled the wood smoke that rose in a blue curl from one of the chimneys.

From the lowest terrace came a harsh cry, and she saw a wonderful, brilliant thing unfurl. A peacock's tail.

"Richard!" Clare gasped, unmoving, still staring. "This house . . . this perfect place. And no one told us it was here, beyond Roman's Grove."

3

THE HOUSE

There was no answer from Richard, so she turned at last and saw her brother standing just outside the trees. His eyes were wide open, but they looked blind. In terror and shock Clare cried: "What's the matter, Rich?"

"I . . . Where are you? I can't see!" he said.

She walked back, took his hand, and spoke words that came unbidden, instinctively, though she did not understand them, or why she was filled with such urgency.

"Richard, of course you can see. Come with me. Come on. *Look at the house!*"

Then the blind look gave place to awareness and intelligence again, and Richard drew a long breath.

"What happened? Must have been too hot, and then coming into the sun. Oh, Clare, what a place! A manor house, isn't it? Whoever thought it would be here?"

Moored to a post on the other side of the lake was a blue boat, and there was someone on the second terrace, which, beyond its balustrade, seemed to be a formal garden. The trees continued along the side of the estate, and Clare and Richard quickly moved into the shadow of leaves, then went slowly on, drawing nearer. It was a girl on the terrace, a girl of around Clare's age, and she was playing with a small white terrier. She wore a long yellow dress under an old-fashioned brown pinafore, and, as she jumped, throwing a ball, they saw that she was wearing boots. On her head was a wide-brimmed straw hat, with a yellow ribbon. Her hair fell on her shoulders in ringlets. It was red hair, vivid in the sunlight that lay full across the terrace.

"Don't let her see us," Clare whispered. "We're trespassing. And these trees aren't very thick. Just a kind of finger of woodland, stretching out from Roman's Grove."

They drew back behind some low branches and watched. The girl sat on the low stone balustrade, tossing up the red ball and catching it, while the little dog leaped, barking.

"She's been to one of those junk places you were so fond of," Richard murmured. "Remember when you bought a weird red dress, all frills and puffed sleeves and down to your feet?"

"And Mother made me throw it away. She wouldn't let me have it cleaned and wear it. It was a pity; I loved that old dress. Of course you can buy something like that new, but it isn't the same. Heaps of girls wear them. But not . . . not holland pinafores."

"Holland? What's that?"

Clare frowned.

"I'm not sure. It looks like it, somehow. In old books.
I never knew what holland was, really, except that it was
brownish. Perhaps she's going to act in a play. Ringlets
. . . I don't like them. I like smooth, straight hair." Her
voice was very low, a little puzzled. The scene, shimmering slightly in the intense heat, was definitely real, but
nonetheless gave a hallucinatory effect. Though there
was sound and smell. Yes, it *was* real.

Clare began to edge onward, following the rise and
keeping just within the trees. This was the back of the
house, or perhaps the side. There must be a front entrance somewhere. Anyway, they had better get out of
sight of the girl.

Leaving the shelter of the trees, they entered a kind
of shrubbery, which still offered fairly safe cover. And
soon they came to a sweep of driveway and were within
sight of what must be the main entrance. There was an
elaborate stone porch, with carvings and a date . . . 1585.
The great studded door was standing half open.

Suddenly there was the sound of horse's hooves and
they ducked down behind a laurel bush just in time.
Around the curve of the driveway came a sleek brown
pony, drawing a large trap with shining brass fittings.
The reins were held by a man wearing dark green livery,
and behind him sat a man—a *gentleman*—in a dark suit,
a high white collar and a top hat. As the pony stopped,
the driver sprang down and held out a deferential hand.
Slowly the man in the top hat stepped to the ground,
and they saw he was carrying a kind of briefcase. The
servant reached into the trap and brought out a large

portmanteau. The word came involuntarily into Clare's mind, though she had never seen one before. A big leather bag, with a fastening on top.

And then the man, the master of the house, turned toward the front door. There was a barking and the sound of running feet, and the white dog and the girl with red hair came bursting around the corner.

"Papa! Papa! You're back! Did you have a good journey? Was the train on time? Was it very hot in London?"

"Oh, there you are, Emily!" he said, kissing her cheek. He sounded a little testy and looked very hot. He put the fingers of his right hand under his collar. "Yes, it was indeed very warm in town, and the drive seemed long from Painsden. I'm glad to be home. You ought not to be running around in the sun. Why aren't you doing your lessons?"

She pouted. She was an attractive girl, but there were lines of discontent on her face.

"It's three o'clock, Papa. I've finished my lessons. And they were just as boring as usual."

Richard glanced at his watch. It was four o'clock, not three. They had taken a long time to get through Roman's Grove; it couldn't really be very far.

"You should be practicing the piano, then. I said that I wished your days to be well filled. I must speak to Miss Grace again."

"She has a headache. She's lying down. I'll practice later, Papa. I wish *I* could go to London again. I wish you'd open our house in Grosvenor Square. There is much more to do in London."

"Not in summer, child. No one stays in London at

this time of year. You know that." He was edging toward the front door. "Where is your mother?"

"Lying down also. Papa, what I really want is to go to boarding school. I've been thinking about it so much lately."

He was beginning to look really irritable.

"That is enough, Emily. You know I won't even consider such a proposition."

"Then at least may I swim in the lake? It's so hot. I have my bathing suit that I wore when we went to Hastings."

"Of course not, child. It wouldn't be suitable. Don't make such suggestions. You sound like your Aunt Ada. Find an improving book, not one of those novels I caught you with last week, and go and sit quietly in the shade. Oh, Blake, is that you?" His tone was one of acute relief as a deferential man in black appeared, took the briefcase and portmanteau and stood back to let his master enter the house. Emily shrugged, pulled a face and retreated back around the house.

The voices, which had been so clear, had all died away, and a hot silence enveloped the whole scene. Even the pony and trap had been driven away, the man in green livery grinning to himself as he caught some of Emily's indiscreet appeals.

"They must have been *acting*," said Richard, and looked around for hidden television cameras. He could see nothing but the sunbaked gravel and the dark green shrubs among which they stood.

"Let's go on," Clare whispered. They followed the driveway for a short distance and then took an offshoot that led to a great stone gateway. The double wooden doors were open and beyond was a stable yard, with old, shining cobblestones. Peering in, they could see a high building opposite, also with double doors thrown back, and inside was something they had only seen in movies or on television . . . a huge carriage, the shafts lying on the ground facing them. There were several sounds; the jingling of harness, the stamping of horses' feet from the stables on their right, the cooing of pigeons. Through another door they could see a man in his shirt sleeves, wearing a coarse sacking apron, polishing something. Then there were footsteps, and the man in green livery appeared. He was tall and dark haired, with heavy features.

"Where's that darn lazy lad?" he shouted.

"About somewhere," said the man in the sacking apron. "I keep at 'im."

"He's to rub the pony down at once. See he does. He ain't worth his keep and half a crown a week."

He climbed some steps on the outside of one of the buildings and disappeared, and the man in the sacking apron began to peer into loose boxes shouting: "Hey you, Tim Moult!" After two or three minutes he gave a yell of fury and reappeared, dragging a small figure after him.

"Asleep! You ain't paid for that. Sleeping in the straw at three o'clock of an afternoon. Well, I've 'ad enough. It's a good whipping you'll get, then you can rub down the pony."

Still holding the writhing small figure, he reached into the room where he had been polishing harness, and his hand came out holding a horse whip.

The boy screamed. The sound echoed around the big,

sunlit yard, and some pigeons rose from a high roof. He was a thin, dark-haired boy, about twelve, wearing ragged trousers and a torn shirt.

"You leave me alone, see! I'll tell me mother!"

"And I'll tell Sir Alan that you're a lazy good for nothing that only deserves a whipping. What d'you think your mother can do, ye young idiot? Dependent on Sir Alan for every blinking thing, the whole family of ye. Take that! An' that!" The whip descended with short, sharp lashes on the boy's defenseless shoulders and back, and he writhed and screamed in agony.

Richard and Clare, gripping hot hands, breathing hard, stared from the dreadful scene into each other's eyes.

"They *must* be acting!" said Richard. "It must be some kind of television thing. But . . ."

"It's not! It can't be. It's real, and that boy will be killed." For there was blood on the boy's back, spreading redly over the dirty white of his shirt, and his pale face was twisted, beaded with sweat. "We've got to stop it!"

"All right!" Richard stepped forward from the shadows of the gateway into the glare of the sun. He shouted, "Stop it at once! How dare you be so brutal? We'll report you to the police."

The man went on lashing, the boy continued to scream, and the pigeons fluttered and cooed on the ledge of a high granary window.

"Maybe that'll teach you, Tim Moult! Get on with yer work." And the boy was flung away until he lay on the cobblestones. The man, furling the whip, walked away into the harness room, and Richard and Clare were

left standing there, blankly, hopelessly bewildered.

Then Clare did move. She went over to the boy and bent over him. "Look, are you all right? Did that brute? ..."

He did not hear. He just lay there in the heat, sobbing, with the blood spreading on his shirt, and suddenly the smell of horse dung and the glare of the sun made Clare feel sick.

The boy did not hear, and the man had not heard. Nor had they been seen. Something was unreal, either them or the stable yard scene, the injured boy. There were no television cameras. Slowly she began to wonder. Could they ... was it possible that they had wandered into another world? And what kind of a world was it where little boys could be beaten nearly to death, and where their mothers had no rights? It was terrifying.

She looked up and said: "Rich, I'm scared! We aren't here ... I mean, they don't know we're here. Something's happened to us. Where are we?"

"Yes, we've come somewhere strange," her brother agreed. It was obvious that there was no acting, no cameras. The boy really was bleeding and lying there on the hot stones, murmuring: "I want me mother!" in a young, sobbing voice with a country accent.

Clare bent again over the boy. She could smell his sweat and see the blood oozing steadily through his shirt. The nape of his neck was very young and delicate, and his hair looked as if it was never combed. But it was short, as if someone had taken shears, not scissors, to cut it.

"Touch him, can you?" said Richard.

Clare put out a hand, then drew it back. The boy looked solid; it would, in a way, have been less terrifying if he had lacked substance. But she couldn't try to touch him.

"We ought to help," she whispered. "We ought to *do* something. Find his mother, or confront that Sir Alan person, but . . ."

"We can't alter it," Richard said. "I think it's something that's already happened. And he won't die. Look! He's moving."

The boy wriggled, raised himself on his elbows, then slowly rose and shuffled away toward a loose box, still sobbing and murmuring about his mother.

Richard put his hot hand on Clare's equally hot arm and steered her out of the stable yard. She went reluctantly, looking over her shoulder.

"You mean to say . . ." She was trying to think. "That things that have happened in the past can't be altered? We might have *stopped* that man beating him. Surely we could have."

"He couldn't see or hear us. If we could really have got through, maybe we might have altered things. I don't know."

"But you do believe that we've got somewhere else?"

"I suppose I do. Or maybe it's the heat."

They seemed to have missed the turning into the drive, for they came, suddenly, onto another yard, where washing hung out to dry. Clare, seeing the things on the clothesline, gave a hysterical giggle.

"Richard, we couldn't be imagining it! Is that a nightgown? Why, it would hold St. Paul's Cathedral! And those great knickers. The long print dresses, and *look* at the aprons! Oh!" For there was someone standing in an open doorway . . . the kitchen doorway, it seemed to be. She was a big woman, with a hard, red-skinned face. She wore a blue-and-white print dress, a white apron similar to the ones on the line and a white cap.

She turned back to shout over her shoulder: "Get on with it, girl! There're all them vegetables to be prepared for dinner, and tea first. Sir Alan's back from London. You wasn't engaged to sit sniveling. You'll feel the flat of my hand again if . . ."

And then, so suddenly that the cook herself was taken by surprise, a figure pushed past her and jumped down the two steps into the yard. She was small and dark-haired, but she might have been thirteen or fourteen. She wore a cotton dress and a rather dirty apron, and she had been crying. Across one cheek a big red mark was rising.

"I'm going 'ome, Mrs. Brewer! I 'ate it 'ere! An' Tim 'ates it, too. I bin workin' since five this morning, and I've cut me finger and I'm going *'ome!*"

The big woman—the cook—moved surprisingly quickly. She seized the girl by the shoulder, spun her around, and pushed her back up the steps.

"You'll do no such thing, Jenny Moult. There's work to be done. You ain't earning your money and keep. Five shillings a week for the likes of you. Cottage trash, and yer ma has five other mouths to feed. Be grateful that Lady Roman decided to employ you. What'd happen to you else, tell me that?"

And then they had both gone back into the kitchen. There was a glimpse of a huge room, with old oak beams, a big table, shining pans and big white bowls. In the background, as the cook moved her bulging body to one side, Clare saw an older girl, her hand over her mouth as if to stifle unkind laughter at poor Jenny's fate.

If that were the case, she soon had to look after herself.

"Now then, you. Ellen! You're not much better than Jenny. Idle as they come. Did you see that the master's hot water went up?"

"Yes, Mrs. Brewer. And . . ."

"Get the tea trays ready, then. Jenny, you help her, and let's have no more nonsense. I'll be mistress in my own kitchen, and neither of you forget it. You know the strength of my hand."

"Horrible old brute!" Clare muttered. She was white faced and shaking, and Richard felt he couldn't stand any more. He steered her out of the yard, and they managed to find the way to the drive and the path through the shrubbery. "Rich, she was his sister. That boy in the stable yard. Five shillings a week, and started work at five, and she's younger than me. What would Father say?"

Her brother didn't answer. Slowly, silently, half in a dream, they edged their way through the trees, making for Roman's Grove. The terraces were quite deserted now, the blue boat was motionless and empty on the lake.

And then they reached the path that led back into the depths of the wood. Clare stopped and looked around at the manor. "It's still there," she said.

The house rose, golden and lovely, wholly real.

"Come *on!*" Richard urged.

"But what if we're in this time forever?"

"We won't be. We'll go through the wood. It'll be all right."

"I can't go far. Not yet. I'm shaking still. Let's sit on this bank . . . Oh, I'm glad to be in the shade. Richard, what *was* it? What *did* it?"

Richard sat down beside her, frowning. His thin fingers picked delicately at a leaf.

"I can't imagine why, if we were going to go back," he said, "we didn't go to Roman times. That's what we were thinking about. Mind you, I never in my wildest dreams thought one *could*. But it was the Roman civilization in Britain that was so close—if it had happened at the villa . . ."

"I wasn't thinking about the Romans," said Clare. "Not really. I can't think that far back. In a kind of a way I've been thinking of times when people rode in carriages, and poorer people had to curtsy and open gates, and be *humble*. So I guess I did it. If one of us did. I dragged you through. You know, Rich, that moment when you couldn't see. It must have been I who took us there, somehow. But I don't know why, or what did it. And *when* was it? Hundreds of years ago?"

"No," he said. "She asked if the train was on time. That red-haired girl, Emily. And there were trains . . . Oh, well, from the middle of the nineteenth century, I think. But I don't think it was as far back as that. She wanted to go to boarding school and swim in the lake."

"But didn't children go to boarding school a long, long time ago? The Brontë sisters did, and that was before . . ."

"I know. But I think it may have been around 1890, or even later."

"But who *are* they? They seem all powerful, the people who live in the house. Sir Alan, that man in the stable yard said, and that cook person said Lady Roman. But the Romans live on the other side of the valley. At least, they do now. I thought the new house was built on the site of the old one." Clare had grown calmer as she tried to work out the mystery.

"No one actually said so. But the man we saw wasn't Lord Romansgrove's *father*. He must have been the first Lord Romansgrove. And this was Sir Alan."

"But perhaps before he got the new title." She was still trying desperately to come to terms with the thing that had happened.

"I really think earlier than that. It must have been before the First World War. Those clothes . . . the trap and the carriage. I'd say somewhere between 1890 and . . . oh, 1910. All powerful, you said. Pretty feudal."

"I'm rested now, so let's go on. I want to see what happens. I'm afraid we might be ghosts, Richard. We must make sure we can get back to . . . to our own time."

"Time!" Richard exclaimed, as they started to walk again. "I looked at my watch, and it was an hour later than they said. They didn't have summer time until the First World War, I'm fairly sure. So definitely before that."

They plunged on through the dark green of the wood, in a panic now, afraid that they might never get out of the past and find their own familiar world.

4

BACK TO
ROMAN'S GROVE

They were very tired, and the struggle through the wood seemed never ending. Bracken and brambles, low branches blocking their way, and, in the motionless heat of late afternoon, the flies were torture.

"We should be out by now," Clare wailed suddenly. "I know we should. We should have seen the valley; come to the stile. Rich, we . . ."

Richard had stopped, too, and was staring around. The sunlight fell in small patches, dazzling in the encircling gloom. In the distance wood pigeons cooed, and the gentle sound seemed almost mocking.

"Wait a minute, Clare. Think! We've been silly, going on like this. At some point we should have turned left.

Don't you remember? We crossed the stile and headed into the wood, then we reached this path and turned *right*. So . . ."

"You mean we've gone past the turning? Yes, of course. It can't have been very clear. We just pushed our way through." Clare fought down panic and tried to be sensible.

"Yes. And it's no good going back. We might not find it. We shall just have to keep on. It's the main path, after all. The wood must end somewhere."

"I think it could go on forever, and we're condemned to keep on through a green gloom . . ."

"Don't be silly. Come on."

They went on, and suddenly, after five minutes or so, the trees thinned ahead and there was a broad sweep of sunlight. They came out on to the edge of the low ridge, and saw the valley spread out below them. The village was directly in front of them, so clearly they had come past the path that led straight across the fields to their own home. Their figuring had been right.

For a moment of sheer terror Clare stared at the scene, wondering, wanting it to be the place they knew. Then she flung herself down at the edge of the bracken. The turf was short and scattered with little clumps of sweet-smelling thyme.

"Oh, Richard!" she cried. "It's all right. See the combine harvester in that field across the valley? And there are . . ."

"Television aerials," said her brother. "And all the newer houses. There's Romansgrove House on the opposite slope."

"So we *are* back? Oh, thank goodness! I thought we'd never see Father and Mother again." She lay flat on the grass, waving a bracken frond to keep off the flies. "Was it a dream, Rich? But, in that case, you dreamed it, too. And the house and people seemed so real."

"I don't think it was a dream," her brother said seriously. "I think we really were there, somehow. The people *were* so real. That girl, Emily, and her arrogant father . . . and the two Moults . . . and the men . . . we couldn't have dreamed all that."

"And the cook, Mrs. Brewer. Those clothes! Richard, if we go back again . . ."

He stared at her. She was dirty and very hot, and her hair was tangled, with leaves and bits of stick caught in it.

"Clare, I thought you were scared? Go back . . . It would be more reasonable if you never wanted to enter Roman's Grove again."

"Yes, it would, wouldn't it?" Clare rose slowly and the scent of crushed thyme was very strong. "But now that I know we *can* get back to our own time, I . . . Well, I'm curious. That girl Emily kind of interests me, wanting to go to school and to swim, and bored with her governess. I suppose Miss Grace *was* her governess? And who was her Aunt Ada? And what happened to the Moults?"

"I know. But look, Clare, it has to be a secret, don't you think?" They were walking on again, following a faint path down the slope, heading for a stile. It looked as if they would come out near South Farm.

"Yes. Our summer secret," Clare said dreamily. "I

suppose we shouldn't have secrets from our parents, but you *can't* tell everything. And this is just too odd. Things are only just starting to get better, and we really mustn't worry them. They'd take us to a doctor first thing tomorrow. We'll decide later if we're going back. Just now I'm really thankful to see this modern world."

The stile led them into a field where the oats had already been cut, and then through two pasture fields, though luckily the cows were at the far side under some trees. Neither was used to cows, though neither would have confessed to being scared. Finally they found themselves in a narrow lane, festooned with honeysuckle and foxgloves. They turned left, passing the gate of South Farm, and hoped soon to reach the village.

Suddenly they heard a shrill whistling, and a boy came around the next bend. He was about Richard's age, well built and suntanned, and he wore a clean white shirt and gray shorts. He grinned as he approached.

"Hello!"

"Hello!" answered Richard. Clare said nothing, merely stared, for the boy reminded her of someone.

"Will this lane take us to Romansgrove village?" Richard asked. He was pretty sure it would, but it seemed necessary to say something.

"Yes. It's just around the next corner." The strange boy sounded friendly. "You been lost?" He was eyeing their hot and grubby appearance. "You don't live around here?"

"Yes, we do. We've come to live in South Lodge. Our name is Manley. Richard and Clare."

"Oh, your father is the new chap in the estate office?

I'm Tom Moult. I live in one of the cottages on the village green. *My* dad is head cowman at South Farm."

"Tom *Moult!*" Clare knew then that he reminded her of the suffering boy in the stable yard, Tim Moult. Tom was better grown, but there was a definite resemblance.

"Yes. What's the matter? You look as if I'm a ghost. There are plenty of Moults around here. Hey, did you get sunstroke or something? Where you been?"

"Lost in Roman's Grove," said Richard, with commendable calm. "We thought we'd never find our way out. We were exploring. Do you ever go there?"

The boy scratched his ear and grinned again.

"Sometimes I take me dog. There're rabbits, and his Lordship doesn't mind. It's an eerie, lostlike place; most people don't like it, but Gran says I've no imagination. My teacher says the same. But why should I have? I'm going to be a cowman like me dad. You don't need imagination with cows. Once I spent a whole night in the ruined house."

"The ruined *house?*"

"Yes. It got late and then it thundered, so me and Billy just waited there until morning. You get that far?"

"I don't know . . ." Clare stammered.

"You'd know if you saw it. Well, I must get on . . . see my friend in Chaneworth. That's the next village. Good-bye." And he was gone, whistling again.

The two Manleys continued to stand in the lane, staring at each other.

"He . . . he must be an ancestor of that boy," Clare whispered.

"Don't you mean descendant?" Richard asked.

"Yes, of course. How silly of me. But I'm beat. A ruined house! It *wasn't* ruined. Great and glorious, but with . . . with awful wrong things going on. Richard, your face is dirty. Do wipe it. And here, I've a little comb in my pocket."

"Your face is dirty, too. And take those bits out of your hair. We can't be seen in the village looking like this."

They did a hasty toilet and walked on. The village of Romansgrove was golden and quiet in the peace of early evening, with just a few people standing talking here and there, and one man cutting the grass outside his garden hedge. They circled the duck pond and passed the estate office, which was closed. It was nearly six o'clock.

Clare's face was very thoughtful; grave and a little sad.

"Rich, what's real? How can we be sure we're real now? I *feel* real, and Tom Moult spoke to us, and those other people smiled at us. But how can we be sure?"

"I don't know what reality is," her brother said. "I imagine people cleverer than we are have asked that question. After all, those others seemed real, too . . . the people at the Manor."

"Shall we be walking along this lane forever, in some part of time?"

"Maybe. There are all kinds of theories about time," Richard said thoughtfully. "I wish I knew more about them. I never paid much attention. I think one is that it's a kind of ribbon, going on forever. So you can go backward or forward, because it's all there. I did read some 'time' plays last term, by J. B. Priestley. They were interesting."

"You didn't tell me," Clare said, almost jealously.

"Well, I suppose it didn't seem important . . . *then*. One was called *I Have Been Here Before*, and another was *Time and the Conways*. Three plays in an old paperback I picked up in school."

"I wish I could read them."

"You probably can, when we join a library here. They're sure to have plenty of old plays. If not we'll find something else. But we'd better not talk anymore now. We're almost home."

"Yes. And I'm not afraid of going home anymore, are you? It was so awful going home after school for all those months; never knowing what Father would be like. But I think things are going to be all right now."

When they entered South Lodge, their father and mother were sitting at the table in the living room, and there was an air of peace and relaxation. Mr. Manley stopped talking to look up at them.

"We were just growing worried. You do look hot. Where did you go? Exploring?"

"Yes, Dad." Clare suddenly realized that she was ravenously hungry. The smell of food made her mouth water. "How was it? Did you find it hard work?"

Mr. Manley began to tell them about his day, while their mother went out to the kitchen to get food for the new arrivals. Over her shoulder she said: "Get washed, do. You both look filthy. And you must be starving."

But for a few minutes they lingered to listen. Both were deeply relieved to see that their father was really relaxed, and seemed happy.

"It *is* an interesting place," he said, "and remarkably well run. I don't think I shall find the work too hard, and it's such a joy to be able to walk to and from work. I had lunch at the Roman Arms. They do excellent food at the bar. And . . ."

"Get washed, you two," their mother said sternly. "Your meal will be cold if you don't hurry."

Clare and Richard fled to the bathroom. Clare whispered: "I'm *sure* it will be all right. He's quite different already. Oh, I *am* so hungry!"

They came downstairs again and sat at the table. There the strange adventure in Roman's Grove really did seem a dream. It was hard to believe it had all happened. And maybe, Clare reflected, it hadn't. When the table was cleared and the dishes washed, Clare fished the pendant out of her pocket and displayed it.

"I found it in the Grove, Mother. It must have been there for years; see how dirty it is. Is there any silver polish?"

Mrs. Manley looked at the pendant with interest.

"It certainly is dirty, but the design is attractive. I think the polish is in the bottom closet in the kitchen."

As she polished, Clare thought again about their extraordinary experience. The house, the lake and the terraced gardens were vivid in her mind. The blue boat, and the girl playing with the dog . . . the very sound of her voice as she talked to her father by the door. She tried not to remember the stark horror of the scene in the stable yard. Yet had it happened really? Or had it been a sort of hallucination?

After much rubbing, the pendant began to shine. It was not pewter, or some other dull material, but looked like silver. Though the long exposure to damp and earth had damaged part of the pattern beyond hope, many of the leaves and flowers stood out clearly.

"I don't suppose there's any chance of finding the owner," said Mrs. Manley, returning to the kitchen to find Clare putting away the polish and cloths. "Of course, if anyone claims it, you'll have to give it back. But otherwise perhaps we could get a new chain for it. Girls often wear these dangly things nowadays."

"I'd like that." Clare was starting up the stairs, with the pendant in her hand. Her mother had followed her to the bottom of the flight.

"Are you all right, Clare?" she asked. "You look very flushed. So does Richard. Too much sun, maybe."

"It *was* hot, but I'm fine," said Clare. She escaped to her bedroom and put the pendant carefully away in a little carved wooden box where she kept an old coral necklace, a silver bracelet and some other treasures. Then she looked at herself in the mirror. She *was* rather pink, and there was a scratch on her cheek. Scratches on her arms, too. Roman's Grove . . . overgrown and secret and strange, the branches catching at them as they tried to pass, brambles holding them back.

Her mother had followed her up the stairs and now she entered the room, holding a small tube.

"Something to soothe those scratches, Clare dear." She lingered for a few moments, and Clare felt uneasy. Her mother obviously sensed something, but how could one say: "Mother, we went back into the past. We saw a wonderful old house, and a pony trap and a great carriage. And *people* . . . real people."

No, of course she couldn't say that.

In a way it was a strange evening, yet peaceful. Mr. and Mrs. Manley sat out on the tiny patch of lawn in front, and there were no feelings of tension coming from them. It seemed a miracle after the terrible months. Almost more of a miracle, Clare decided, than their afternoon adventures. She and Richard, who had both had enough sun, wandered around doing small jobs. Richard was still putting his possessions in order, and he occasionally stopped to strum on his guitar. Clare sorted out the family books and began to put them in place. Her own she had done already; they were all up in her room, in their usual order. Clare was meticulous about books.

Once, when they met on the landing, Clare whispered: "Our summer secret. Mother feels there's something."

"I know," her brother murmured back. "But we can't possibly tell. What are we going to do tomorrow?"

Clare laughed and looked out the window at the top of the stairs, to where Roman's Grove lay dark and waiting against the evening sky.

"I am afraid of it," she said. "And yet . . . we did get back safely."

"You're willing to go again? In the morning?"

"Why not? We know the way now, and next time we'll mark the point where the side path goes in. It won't be so tangly, either, for we broke branches and crushed down bracken. We could go soon as we've had breakfast and made our beds. Unless Mother wants us to do something special."

Richard, too, looked across the valley to Roman's Grove. It *had* been fascinating. And that red-haired girl, Emily, was interesting; a bit of a rebel. Girls must have led very dull lives then. Emily and the other people they had seen had seemed so real, . . . not in the least like ghosts. Come to that, which of them had been the ghosts? If time *was* a kind of ribbon, already imprinted with events, it had all happened, but still it would be happening forever. Thinking of it gave him a slight headache, and he was glad to have his attention arrested by another voice below. Lady Romansgrove had arrived.

Mrs. Manley was bringing another chair, and Lady Romansgrove, wearing a plain green dress this time, was talking cheerfully. Her voice came up to them:

"My daughter Victoria will be home in a day or two. I miss her when she's away. My son, Alan, who is sixteen, is hitchhiking in France somewhere. My husband is bitterly against hitchhiking. He says it's begging, and dangerous as well, but Alan just laughs. He's nearly six feet tall and very tough. In September next year he's going to an agricultural college. Meanwhile, he's still at school."

"When he's finished college, will he help to run the estate?" Mr. Manley asked.

"Oh, yes. He may take over one of the farms. Mr. Bradley at East Farm is getting old. He'll want to retire in a few years. Alan's a good worker. He's been working around the estate since he was ten. We all keep at it. This is just a short holiday for him."

Clare and Richard, listening at the open window, exchanged glances. The Romans obviously were not idle. That ought to placate their father, and in both their minds were pictures of that spoiled, rather resentful girl, Emily Roman, who had probably never done anything useful in her life. But it was not her fault; she was not expected to work. *Those* Romans had taken it for granted that their employees should do it all, for a pittance of a wage.

"But where does Emily come in?" Clare asked, as she and Richard went together into her bedroom. "She was a Roman, but . . . but if she married she would have another name. She must have had a brother who inherited the estate."

"Try asking her in the morning," said Richard, grinning.

"You know she won't be able to see or hear us. That's a bore, having no contact," Clare grumbled. "*We* could see and hear and smell. And yet we didn't seem to be there for *them*."

"Well maybe there's another way to find out," said Richard. "So all right. We'll go after breakfast."

"I don't know how long this wonderful weather will last," said Mrs. Manley, on Friday morning, after her husband had walked off, in a leisurely way, to the estate office. "It's hotter than ever. There's a bus to Painsden at 9:30, so I think I'll go and see what stores there are and have coffee; I'll come back on the twelve o'clock bus. There are more buses on Fridays. We'll have a cold lunch at one, and your father's coming back for that. What will you do? Do you want to come with me?"

"If you don't mind, Mother, we'd sooner go out walking," Clare said hurriedly. "If . . . if you won't be lonely."

"No, do as you like. I expect Painsden will be very crowded, since it's market day. I thought I might call in at the town hall and see what chance there is of some teaching in September. Not full-time, perhaps, but it would be easy, really. I can have the car now your father isn't using it."

"So why the bus this morning?" Richard asked.

"Oh, to meet people. I expect half the village goes into town on Friday."

She left at 9:15 to walk to the village, for the bus left from outside the Roman Arms. Five minutes later Clare and Richard locked the back door, as instructed, and, in silence, climbed the stile and set off across the sun-drenched fields to the dark grove on the ridge.

It seemed much quicker the second time. They plunged into the wood without hesitation and certainly found the going easier. When they reached the main path, Richard paused to collect a few stones and a long branch, and made a big arrow pointing to the way they had come. Then, mainly silent still, they set off through the great wood. When they had walked for some time, and were past the remains of the Roman villa and the place where she had found the pendant, Clare said:

"I'm scared and excited . . . Richard, aren't you? I want it to happen again, yet I'm afraid."

Richard nodded. "Do you want to go on? We *could*

turn back and forget it."

"Oh, but we can't do that! We're nearly there. And we must see Emily again. *When* do you think we go back? Just when we come to the end of the wood or before?"

Her brother shook his head. "I haven't the slightest idea. Maybe at the point where we see the house. It must be soon now."

And then they pushed their way out into the blazing sunlight, and Clare, slightly ahead, stopped and stared in blank dismay and astonishment. She stood there, flies buzzing around her head, and sticking to her hot arms. It had all been for nothing. They would not see Emily or anyone else. They were all gone.

5

THE GIRL
IN THE BOAT

Richard pushed his way through the last of the bracken and reached her side.

"Oh!" he gasped. And then: "I don't understand! It's a different place."

"No," said Clare. "The same place. That boy, Tom Moult, said there was a ruined house."

Ahead of them was high grass and bushes, with no sign of a lake, though there were bulrushes and reeds in a hollow. The tall brown heads of the bulrushes were moving gently in the hot breeze.

Where the terraces had been, with low balustrades of golden stone and peacocks strutting splendidly, there was now only an overgrown slope on which a few stones showed here and there. And the house . . . that beautiful old house, with its mullioned windows, its lovely golden gables and Tudor chimneys. Its glory was all gone, and all they saw at the top of the rise were walls overgrown with ivy. There were no chimneys, and the whole house was roofless. At the extreme eastern end there were only the lower walls, but half the house still stood to almost its full height. One broken gable held a window space through which the sky was visible. Over most of it the encroaching ivy had made a dark green covering. Like a pall, Richard thought. And wondered why he had had such a strange thought. But the house was dead . . . quite dead.

"We didn't go back," Clare whispered. "This is how it is now. They're all dead and gone. Emily, and her father, and that boy called Tim Moult. Oh, Rich!" There was infinite sadness in her voice. "It wasn't real. And now I know how much I wanted to see it again. Most of all I wanted to see Emily and try to know her."

"Let's go nearer," her brother said, and he began to lead the way through the hot, secret silence. The place seemed so alone now, so forsaken. Perhaps only the modern Tom Moult and his dog, Billy, ever came there. They climbed the slope where the terraces had been. In the tangle of growth Clare suddenly stumbled over a broken statue.

"I don't think I can bear it!" she murmured. "What *happened* to them?"

Richard had reached the highest point, where once the topmost terrace had been, immediately outside the house. Now it was a mass of nettles and brambles, but he moved slowly until he could push aside a patch of ivy here and there and examine the remaining wall.

"I think the house burned," he said. "There are marks on all these stones, underneath the ivy. The stone is almost black . . . look! I don't believe time would do that; not in a place where the air is so clean."

"Burned!" Clare came to look. "Oh, but, Rich . . . Then what happened to *them?*"

"I don't know. Maybe we'll find out. Come on."

They walked slowly around the shell of the house and found the weed-grown driveway and the remains of the old front porch. Here Sir Alan Roman had talked to his daughter and then had entered a real, living house. Now the way was blocked by thick brambles and ivy, and a flourishing honeysuckle hung down over the date stone. Richard pulled the trails of flowers aside, and the date was still there . . . 1585.

"We couldn't get in here," he said. "That ivy is as thick as my wrist."

Clare shuddered. "I don't want to go in."

"Are you sure?" Richard asked. "I think we could manage it back there on the terrace. There was a big gap near where I was looking at the burned stone. Where a window had been, I suppose. The ivy made a kind of hanging curtain there, and it would push aside."

"I'd *hate* to go in!" Clare said vehemently.

"Well, so would I, really. And it might not be very safe. All right, come on. Let's see what else is left."

Silently, slowly, they moved on until they found the remains of the great stable yard. The entrance was still there, intact, but the buildings were crumbling. They had not been burned, but time and weather had taken their toll. The carriage house was the most whole, but there was nothing inside it. Only pigeons, descendants possibly of those they had seen and heard the day before, fluttered and cooed on the broken roof. The cruelty of the man, the agony of the young boy, were both gone. The horses had died long ago. No one cleaned harness anymore in the ruined buildings, but they did find a horsewhip in the grass that almost covered the old cobblestones.

Clare started back from the whip as if it were a snake, and, in fact, it looked a bit like one. But the thongs fell to pieces when Richard lifted it.

"Can it have been the one *he* used?" she gasped. "Rich, I don't think I can bear this."

"They must have had plenty of whips," Richard said grimly.

"But why didn't we go back?" Clare asked fiercely. "I hated some of it, but I *did* want to find out more. Rich, it's just so strange, and I don't understand."

"I don't understand, either," Richard confessed. "Something brought us the first time. As for what happened . . . we could ask."

Clare stood in the hot shadows of the carriage house.

"No, I won't ask How could we? Well, yes, I suppose we could. We could say we found the ruined house. But I don't want to do that. I want to find out some other way. Oh, Richard, I want to go *back*."

"I don't know how," he said.

They began retracing their steps through Roman's Grove, lost in thought. It was Clare who spoke first.

"I've been trying to think of anything that was different that first time," she said. "And nothing was, except that pendant I found. I left it at home today. Richard, could it have been that?"

Richard frowned as he pushed his way through the high bracken.

"You mean . . . maybe it belonged to someone then? And it was the key, the link. It *could* have been, I guess. It might have lain in the wood for a long time. But . . ."

"There *was* something strange about the way I found that pendant. I didn't even want to admit it to myself at the time, but it's true. I felt as if I couldn't move away from that place, and something just made me put my hand into the hole. Did someone then want us to come? Or want something to happen anyway? Emily maybe? She seemed so unhappy."

"It's the only thing, and I have to try. Let's bring the pendant with us and come back this afternoon."

"Do you believe that it's a magic pendant?" Richard sounded a little amused.

"No-o," said Clare. "Not quite that. Just a . . . a connection. It's all I can think of. If you won't come, I'll come alone."

"Really?" He stopped and looked back, eyeing her with respect and a trace of amusement. Not that any of it was really *funny*, but if one took it with absolute seriousness it was just too much. Only, thought Richard, seeing Clare's grave face, it was serious. If the thing went on, if the pendant were the answer, heaven knew where it would end. Maybe he ought to refuse to go. Clare wouldn't really go alone.

"What would happen if you got lost in the wood or in that other time?" he asked.

Clare tossed her head.

"I won't do either. But you *will* come?"

He nodded and went ahead again through the wood. The path was too narrow, and still too tangly, for walking two abreast.

They were back home before their father and mother, and Clare said it was just as well. They weren't as dirty and torn as on the previous day, but they were very hot, and the aura of secrets still hung around them.

"We'll wash quickly," she said. "And start getting the lunch. I'll do the salad. All the things are in the refrigerator. Mother bought them yesterday at the village store. Lettuce, tomatoes, cucumber . . . Oh, and some cold potato. And boiled ham. Quick!"

Fifteen minutes later, when their parents arrived together, Clare was drying lettuce and Richard slicing tomato and cucumber. The table was ready, and the hot flush on both their faces had died down.

"But I do feel guilty," Clare whispered.

"We didn't do anything but walk in the wood."

"Yes, but you know what I mean."

Mrs. Manley had met many local women on the bus and had gleaned a good deal of information and gossip. She recounted some of it as they ate, but Clare and Richard scarcely listened. They were occupied with their own thoughts.

"The Romans seem very popular," Mrs. Manley ended. "Everyone seems to like them, and they all feel a proprietary interest in the estate."

Mr. Manley nodded, both Clare and Richard noted with pleasure. It was going to be all right here.

By two o'clock Clare and Richard were ready to go out again. Clare had given the pendant a long look and then put it in her pocket. It seemed their only hope of going back into that other time. As they both came downstairs Mrs. Manley eyed them anxiously.

"Are you sure it isn't too hot? Don't tire yourselves too much. Why not wait until evening before going out again?"

"But we like the heat, Mother," said Clare. "We want to go now, unless . . . Will you be lonely?"

"No, I shan't be lonely. I met Lady Romansgrove just as I was getting off the bus, and she has promised to bring me some plants this afternoon. They're to put around the edge of the backyard. Of course it's rather hot for putting in anything, but I'll water them in well. It's just so that the low banks won't look so bare, and some of that part is very shady."

"She'll probably help you and stay to tea," said Richard.

His mother laughed.

"She may. She's a very keen gardener, I gather. She looks after the gardens up at the house, doing it all except the heavy digging. They always have homegrown vegetables."

"So Mother's all right," murmured Clare, as they slipped thankfully away.

They went back through the fields and climbed the last stile into the Grove. As Richard said, they would soon be able to do it blindfolded. Each time they went the way seemed shorter, but, as they approached the end of the wood, both walked more slowly. Clare fingered the pendant and tried to throw her thoughts back. If the house was still ruined this time, that was the finish; they would simply have to try to forget yesterday's strange adventure.

But the house was whole. The terraces were there again, and the peacocks, and Richard saw it all at the same moment as Clare. He did not have to be dragged with her this time.

The blue boat was on the lake, and in it sat a girl . . . Emily, wearing a white dress and a big white hat; no holland pinafore. Her back was turned to them and she was reading, or so it seemed. Her head was slightly bent, and they saw her arm move as if to flick over a page.

"Oh, I'm so glad!" Clare gasped, and she really was relieved and delighted to see Emily again, sitting so peacefully in the blue boat on a summer afternoon. The thought of her gone forever had been a curiously painful one. "Though if we get to know her, we may not like her," she added. "Let's go nearer, Rich."

Richard moved forward, glad himself to see the idyllic scene again. The house, the gardens and the little lake had an almost lyrical beauty; yet it was clear from their one short visit that there were cankers at the heart of it all. Physical and probably mental cruelty. It was a wonderful world for the very rich, he thought. They saw the beauty. But it was a pretty difficult place, even a terrible one, for the employed, the poor and the dependent. For them the beauty did not exist at all. Young children could be exploited and beaten, and denied all chances of proper education. The scenes in the stable yard and by the kitchen door were as much a part of all this as Emily in her boat.

"Well, be careful," he cautioned. "Go quietly."

"She can't see us," Clare said, but she spoke softly. "Or hear us. I almost wish she could."

"She'd scream the place down and have us turned off the estate by that awful groom. Beaten, too, most likely."

Even though they knew they were invisible, it shook them to see a figure coming down from the highest terrace near the windows of the house. She was moving quickly and had soon reached the second terrace, then had skimmed down the shallow golden steps to the third. She was grown-up, but in spite of the long, plain brown dress, with its high collar, it was easy to see that she was not very old. Perhaps nineteen or twenty. As she drew nearer, they saw that she was pale and delicate looking, but rather pretty. She was hatless, as if she had come outdoors in a hurry (didn't people always wear hats then?), and her hair was light brown and drawn back from her face. She actually jumped the last three steps to the smooth grass and came hurriedly forward.

Clare and Richard shrank back, feeling terribly real, with the sun on their bare arms and heads, but clearly she couldn't see them.

"Emily!" she cried, as soon as she was near the boat. "Emily, what did I tell you? You haven't practiced that piece, and your mother wants you to play it for her dinner party guests tomorrow evening. It is really too bad of you, sitting there reading one of those unsuitable novels from the library. You are far too young for such writing."

The girl in the boat flung down her book pettishly.

"It isn't a novel. If you want to know, it's a school story Aunt Ada smuggled to me last time she was here. She knows how I feel about school, and these lucky girls in the book play hockey and cricket and go camping. *Camping*. Think of that, Miss Grace. In tents."

"It sounds highly unsuitable. Your Aunt Ada has no right to encourage you. She isn't a woman . . . she's just aping men."

"Well, she enjoys it, and at least she is free, which is more than I am. I know it's rather shocking," Emily admitted. "Wearing bloomers and riding a bicycle, and talking all the time about women's rights. As if women will ever have the vote. Papa says men will always run the country. He gets so angry at her. I know he wishes she wouldn't come here to Romansgrove Manor, but she *is* his sister, and I'm glad she comes. She . . . She scares me; she has such strange ideas. And she never faints like Mama, or seems to want to rest. But she's exciting, too, and she told Papa I *should* be sent away to school. After all, Amy Marlow, on the next estate, goes to a real boarding school and sleeps in a dormitory. She came to tea at Easter and told me all about it. Papa says he doesn't want to quarrel with the Marlows, since they're so rich and important, but all the same he says she must not come again. I asked him last night."

Miss Grace stood on the shore of the lake, staring at the girl in the boat.

"The Marlows have advanced ideas, apparently. Rich girls should be educated at home. You know that your father will never send you to school. He wants you to be gentle and accomplished in the right things."

"Playing that dreadful 'piece'!" Emily said bitterly. "And coming down from the schoolroom for dessert. It's all so boring."

"It may be boring, but you are lazy and disobedient. Come indoors at once, Emily."

Emily turned slightly. Her face under the big white hat was mocking and a little cruel.

"*You* don't want me to go to school, do you, Miss Grace? You only came in May, when Miss Hannah left, but you want to stay at Romansgrove Manor. You have your own reasons, don't you?"

A vivid blush spread slowly over the young woman's pale face.

"How dare you! You . . . you . . ."

"You're rather attracted to the curate, aren't you?" Emily was still mocking, but there was a note of interest and curiosity. "I saw you when I was out riding with Papa . . . standing in the churchyard, talking together. Papa didn't notice, because he was looking the other way. And I've seen you slip out of the house. I think you meet Mr. Baines in Roman's Grove."

"If I do, it's no business of yours. You are being impertinent, Emily." Miss Grace tried to be dignified and didn't succeed very well.

"We-ell, Papa wouldn't like it. If I told him, he would be angry. I'm sure Mr. Baines can't afford to marry until the Vicar retires next year, and Mr. Baines won't get the living if Papa doesn't approve. Papa can arrange things as he wishes. Besides, Mr. Baines comes from a *tainted* family." She shot a malicious glance at the young governess.

"What *do* you mean?" asked poor Miss Grace.

Emily had gone pink in her turn, but she answered boldly:

"He has a brother in a lunatic asylum, and his father was pretty crazy, too. No one can have known that when Mr. Baines was accepted as curate here. Oh, I . . . I overheard someone talking. I couldn't help it. I don't usually listen to the servants' gossip."

"But . . ." Miss Grace looked both stricken and horrified. "I don't believe a word of it. Edgar would have told me. You are a wicked girl. Who was saying such things?"

Emily shrugged.

"It slipped out. I didn't mean to say that. Maybe it isn't true. *But,*" she added, as a final shot, "Papa may never send me to school, but if I say you aren't teaching me well and haven't enough authority, he will get another governess. Papa can be stern, but he spoils me really. If I said . . ."

"You have said enough!" cried Miss Grace. "Stay in your boat. Read your stupid book. I shall tell your mother that you wouldn't practice the piano." And, showing more temper than might, perhaps, have been expected from her appearance, she turned on her heel and almost ran back to the terraces. On the lowest one a peacock gave a loud, mocking cry and spread its wonderful feathers.

"Oh, I say!" gasped Clare. She and Richard had listened in fascination and horror. "She *is* a horrible girl. That was blackmail, and it was cruel." And then, without thinking, but fully believing herself a kind of ghost, she moved quickly until she was within a foot or two of the boat, facing Emily. "I said it was blackmail!" she shouted. "Emily Roman, how could you? Threatening her, and saying those awful things about the curate. And she looks so nice. What if she does love the curate? It's nothing to do with you!"

The shock was enormous. Emily Roman had heard; Emily Roman could see her. Their eyes met, and Emily's mouth dropped open in astonishment and . . . was it fear? No, indignation.

"Who are you?" Emily asked. "How *dare* you!"

Richard joined Clare, and Emily's eyes widened still further. She put out her hand to take the short rope and draw the boat nearer the bank. Then she opened her mouth as if to scream.

"Shut up!" Richard said quickly. "I mean, do please be quiet, Emily. Clare didn't mean to be rude, though you really were unkind to that poor girl. We want to talk to you."

Emily scrambled out of the boat, clasping the school story to her chest.

"Talk to me? But . . . But . . . You have no right here. This is private property. I will . . ."

"Wait!"

"But you must be gypsies. Or . . . Or . . ." Emily's wide eyes stared at them; brown eyes, with light flecks in them. She looked puzzled, but there was an arrogance about her that no girl of the nineteen seventies could ever have assumed.

Clare giggled; it was mostly shock and nervousness. But Richard, in his shabby, sleeveless blue sweater and even shabbier jeans, and she in her old green blouse and jeans, must indeed look like vagrants to this girl with the red ringlets under the big white hat. Her long white dress was spotless, the waist tied with a blue sash.

"Honestly, we're not gypsies," Clare said quickly. "We're Clare and Richard Manley. *She* couldn't see us, but you can . . . It's a kind of miracle. And we *do* want to talk to you. We . . . we'd like to be friends with you; and I'm sorry I spoke so unkindly. Though," she added truthfully, "I did mean what I said. You were horrid to her."

Emily had grown pale, so that a few freckles on her nose suddenly stood out. She seemed to be hesitating between continuing arrogance and fear.

"I—I don't understand," she said slowly. "I shall shout for someone to come. They'll beat you and send you away. How *dare* you speak to me like that? I am Emily Cecilia Victoria Roman, and my father is the most important man for miles and miles. *Far* more important than Sir James Marlow, who owns the next estate. My father owns three thousand acres of land, four farms and the whole village of Romansgrove. He . . . He'll have you flogged."

"Like Tim Moult in the stable yard," said Richard, and Emily stepped back, nearly falling into the lake. "We saw that yesterday. Perhaps you didn't know. Tim Moult doesn't matter to you, and it *isn't* really your

fault. You can't help it. But it's no use calling for anyone. They couldn't see us. At least, no one but you has
seen us so far. You didn't have a chance yesterday; we
were hiding in the shrubbery by the front door when
your father came home. And then we went to the stable
yard and saw that awful thing."

Emily was definitely scared now.

"But . . . Clare and Richard Manley? I thought Clare
was a girl's name. In a way you look like a girl, but your
hair is short and you have . . . have . . ." Her gaze rested
on Clare's blouse, and she went scarlet with embarrass-
ment.

"Breasts," said Clare. "Of course I'm a girl."

"How can you use such a word? Aunt Ada would,
but . . ."

"Your Aunt Ada seems to have all the sense," Richard remarked. "And women got the vote . . . Oh, long
ago. I *think* it was just after the First World War."

"The war's over," Emily whispered. "We beat the
Boers."

"When?" Richard asked, looking interested. They
would find out the date now. The Boer War! It must
have been over by 1900 or 1901. He was not sure.

Emily tossed her head.

"You're trying to trick me. You know it's the summer
of 1902. And I wish you'd tell me why Clare is wearing
trousers and has cut her hair. I suppose she had 'something' in it. Sometimes the heads of the village children
have to be shaved. Of course hers isn't that short, and it
looks shiny and healthy, but . . ."

"I never did!" Clare exploded. "Heaps of girls have

short hair. Others have it long and loose, only never in ringlets. And these are jeans that I'm wearing. They're old, but we came through the wood, and it's very tangly. Listen, Emily, and don't be scared. It's very interesting, really. *I* was scared at first, but now I'm not. If you're going to talk to us some more, you've got to swallow it. Oh, bother! I mean you must try to understand. We're from the future, seventy years and more. And don't ask us how we got here, for we don't really know. We look quite real, don't we? And so do you to us. So *don't* scream and run away. We want to know you."

6

CONVERTING EMILY ROMAN

"I expect the sun was too hot," said Emily. "I should have done my piano practicing. I have sunstroke."

"It *is* hot, but no, you haven't," Clare said briskly. "Only, if you yell and bring someone, they'll certainly think you have. And if you want to know about school, we can tell you. We don't go to boarding school, but we both went to a huge day school in the North. There were more than one thousand boys and girls."

"But there couldn't be!" cried Emily, sounding natural for the first time. "Not a thousand. In this book there were forty girls, and that seemed a great many to me. And you said boys as well as girls. Aunt Ada said they do educate them together in America. Coeducation, they call it. I didn't really believe her. I only know one boy, and he's my cousin. He comes to visit here sometimes, and he teases. I don't like him much. He's nearly sixteen and goes to Eton. I'm fourteen. How . . . How old are you?"

"Clare's nearly fourteen, and I'll be thirteen in two weeks' time," Richard said easily. It was extraordinary how they had settled into conversation.

Emily looked from one to the other and then said: "From the future? If I'm not suffering from sunstroke, it must be some kind of joke. You speak like educated people, so maybe you aren't gypsies. But it is a very absurd joke all the same."

"No, it's true," Clare said. "We found ourselves here yesterday, and we were scared. But still we wanted to come back. And then we saw you in the boat, and heard you being so unkind to poor Miss Grace. Why were you? Don't you like her?"

Emily shrugged, but looked a little ashamed.

"She is just my governess. I don't have to like her. I find her boring. So earnest about lessons and music, but then she wishes to please Papa. It was true about Mr. Baines. I did see her talking to him in the churchyard, and I have also seen her slipping out in the evening with a shawl over her head. She doesn't care about me. She only wants to stay here because of that stupid curate."

"But you were awful to her. Didn't you think of her feelings at all? And what did you mean about a tainted family? All that about being crazy?" Clare asked. "Was it just servants' gossip?"

"I should not have listened, and I should not have said

that to Miss Grace," Emily muttered. "It is beneath my dignity to listen to the servants, but they didn't know I was sitting on the window seat behind the drapes in the drawing room. It was two of the housemaids and Maggie is not a local girl, though she is cousin to a family in the village. I believe she comes from a village ten miles the other side of Painsden, and apparently Mr. Baines' family live near there." She threw up her head and said defiantly: "If it is true, I have done Miss Grace a *kind* deed."

"She doesn't think so," Richard retorted. "You should learn to think of other people. Look! There's someone over there."

A small figure was slipping along at the edge of the grass, heading rapidly for Roman's Grove. At the same moment the sun disappeared behind a cloud and a surprisingly chilly wind suddenly ruffled the waters of the little lake. Emily shivered.

"It's Jenny Moult, I think. A young girl from the village my mother recently engaged as kitchen maid. I shall send her indoors for a shawl." And she called imperiously: "Come here!"

"Yes, it is Jenny," Clare murmured.

Jenny stopped and then came slowly toward the lake. She was without her apron, but still wore her print dress, and her feet were encased in clumsy boots.

"Yes, Miss?" she asked nervously, as she approached.

"Where are you going, Jenny?"

" 'Ome to me mother, Miss Emily. Mrs. Brewer said I could, if I was quick. An' it's quicker through Roman's Grove." The girl dropped a hasty curtsy.

"Well, you can fetch me a shawl first. Ask one of the housemaids to find it for you. I think I left it in the library. Hurry!"

"Yes, Miss Emily. Quick as I can." Jenny was clearly eager to be gone. The unexpected errand would probably leave her little time with her mother, but Emily obviously didn't think of that.

"Jenny!" Emily called after her, and Jenny stopped abruptly, looking scared. "Do you see anyone else here? Am I alone?"

Jenny looked terrified. "Of course, Miss."

"Very well. Bring the shawl."

Jenny scuttled rapidly back in the direction of the house.

"I *must* be suffering from sunstroke," said Emily, staring after her.

"You aren't. Don't worry," Richard said amusedly. "Only from lack of manners."

"What?" Emily looked shocked.

"Don't you ever say 'please'?"

"To the servants? Of course not. They don't expect it."

"You don't need the shawl, anyway," said Clare. "The sun's out again. But now you know *you* can see us, when the others can't. We are here."

Emily dismissed the last two sentences with a puzzled frown.

"The sun may be out, but it will thunder later. She may as well fetch the shawl. I don't see why a girl so newly in our employ should want to go to see her mother. I know the Moults," she said, with a shudder.

"One of our most feckless families. There are six children, and the father, Papa says, is sometimes difficult. Always complaining that their cottage is in bad condition. Most of the cottages are, but good enough for the likes of them."

"They're people," said Richard. "They have some rights."

Emily stared. "They're not important; what rights can they have? They get their wages, and their homes, even if the rain does come through the roof. My papa gets very angry when the village people try to speak to him, ask for better conditions. He could just turn them out; then where would they go?"

Richard laughed. "I think we're going to have to try to convert you, Emily Roman! I wish my father were here. He'd have a few words for you."

Emily looked arrogant again, fear forgotten.

"I am already converted. Do you think we Romans are savages? We go to church twice on Sundays, and all the servants and estate workers have to go at least once. I learn my catechism, and I can repeat whole passages of the Bible from memory."

"I didn't mean that kind of conversion, Emily," Richard said. "Of course you must have been taught to believe in God."

"Naturally," said Emily, wide-eyed. "Everyone believes in God. All decent people believe in God and go to church regularly. My father would dismiss any man who didn't attend at least one service on a Sunday. And of course any woman in his employ also. In summer we have cold meals so that the cook, Mrs. Brewer, may attend both morning and evening service. My father says we must set a good example, and so must the higher servants. *But* my Aunt Ada says some people don't believe . . . or that they have doubts. She says she is an agnostic. Papa nearly said she must never come to Romansgrove Manor again when he heard that, but he didn't quite dare. Aunt Ada would just have laughed. But it is very shocking to be an agnostic, isn't it? She'll go to hell when she dies. As for being an atheist, that is a terrible word. Everyone must be a Christian."

"Our father is an atheist. We never go to church," said Clare. "People are all different, Emily. In our school we had plenty of Jews, and an Arab family, and lots of Pakistanis. They aren't Christians. People can have some other religion, or sometimes they have none at all, and they are just as good as people who have."

"But they'll be damned forever," Emily said, shuddering. "You should hear our vicar when he talks of hellfire. Papa insists on a good sprinkling of hellfire in all the sermons. He says it keeps people up to the mark."

"Can't you see that's very useful?" asked Richard. "Your father wants to keep people cowed. But things change . . ."

"You shouldn't speak of my father like that. We give money to convert the heathen. It is very valuable work."

"It would be better to give people here a living wage and proper roofs over their heads. Sit down on the grass," said Richard. "We'll tell you about Romansgrove now. In our own time, I mean."

Emily gasped, looked like arguing, then obeyed. Jenny Moult came back with the shawl, and Emily took it without a word of thanks. Jenny went off as fast as she could into the gloom of Roman's Grove. Emily gazed after her.

"My mother said she must have footwear. She's been barefoot all her life. We're good to our employees. In winter, or when people are sick, my mother sometimes takes soup to them . . ."

"Like in an old book!" Clare exclaimed. "I never really believed that people did. Are they grateful?"

"But of course they are," said Emily, in a tone that implied "They'd better be, or else . . ." Then, honest again, she added, biting her lip to keep back laughter: "Oh, once it was very terrible! An old woman threw the soup at Mama. I was there, so I saw it. But she was a very old woman, and in her dotage, of course. Papa had her put in an institution in Painsden, and she died soon after."

Clare and Richard exchanged glances.

"I think you'd better listen to us, Emily," said Clare. "Whether you believe it or not. In Romansgrove village now, in *our* time, all the old cottages have bathrooms, and the new estate houses have central heating, and . . ."

"Bathrooms? For cottage people? There are only two bathrooms in the Manor," said Emily, staring up the slope to her home. "You're telling lies, and . . . and I don't believe this talk of another time."

"It's true, all the same."

"But central heating! I know the Romans had it nearly two thousand years ago. They had it in that villa in the Grove. Long ago they found traces of a hypocaust. There was a furnace below, and it sent hot air into their

rooms. The Roman people must have been clever."
Emily sighed. "In winter I always have chilblains, in
spite of the fact that we have big fires. That's one maid's
work, carrying coal up to the bedrooms."

"The poor maid!" said Richard. "And you'll never believe this, but all the workers have rights. If they don't
like things, they can go on strike or appeal to their
unions. But on the Romansgrove estate, in our day,
every worker takes a bonus out of the profits. Oh,
bother! You can't understand, and it's not really your
fault; maybe it's time we stopped this and talked about
something lighter."

Emily did understand in a way, but she was scared
again. She put out her hand and said: "Can you touch
me? Can I touch you?"

"That's something we haven't tried," Clare admitted,
hesitating. The three stared at each other. The chill
breeze had gone and the sun beat down, seeming hotter
than ever. There was a small bead of sweat on Emily's
slightly freckled nose. It was a pretty enough nose,
though perhaps a little too long. She held out her hand,
then drew it back again.

"It *is* a trick of some kind. You may not be gypsies,
but someone has to put you up to this. Someone in the
village, to get better conditions. And of course Jenny
Moult knew."

"No one has. We've told you the truth as we know
it," Richard assured her. "But you do admit the people
need better conditions?"

"Oh, bother the people!" Emily said pettishly. "I
don't believe in ghosts or fairy tales, but I . . . I am

afraid to try and touch you. I *dare* you to touch me."

They had all risen to their feet. Clare was just putting out her brown and not very clean hand to accept the dare when an imperious voice called from the terraces: "Emily, child! I wish to speak to you. Miss Grace tells me . . ."

The spell was broken. Emily looked toward the woman on the golden steps and said hurriedly: "I'll have to go to Mama. But I will not tell her about you. It must be teatime." She glanced at a little watch pinned to her dress. "Nearly four o'clock." And then she saw Clare's wristwatch, which said nearly five o'clock. "What a very curious watch! And it doesn't keep good time."

"Emily, come at once!"

Emily turned her back on her mother before she spoke again, in a low voice.

"I will have to go, but I want to speak to you again. Will you come back tomorrow?"

"We'll try," Clare promised. "But tomorrow's Saturday, and Father may want to take us out somewhere. We'll come soon, anyway."

Emily turned to face her mother and walked slowly away over the smooth grass. Lady Roman was at the foot of the steps by then. She had red hair under a big blue hat, and her dress fell to the ground, with many flounces. She looked and sounded annoyed, as her voice came back to Clare and Richard.

"I wish you to play your piece tomorrow evening, and yet you are so idle and disobedient . . . lazing in the boat, and the sun can't be good for you. And what were you *doing* turning your back on me? Sometimes I think I'll never understand you."

"Poor old Emily!" Clare murmured. "She doesn't seem to have much of a time, and *we* were rather awful to her, talking to her like that. *We* don't preach about hellfire, but we were preaching, all the same."

"Only telling her what's true. But I know what you mean," Richard admitted. "It's so tempting to try to influence her. Yet of course we can't, because this is all long past, and . . . Oh, I don't pretend to understand any of it."

"She does seem so real, though, Rich. It's hard to remember that she must be dead, and the Manor is a ruin. We don't know when it burned . . ."

They had started to walk back toward Roman's Grove. Richard said: "Better not tell Emily what happened to it."

"No-o. We need only say it seems to have been abandoned, and a new house built on the opposite side of the valley. I wonder if we could show it to her? Take her with us, you know. If *we* can come back to her time, maybe we can pull Emily into the future. Only there's one thing, Richard. Don't tell her about the pendant. If it was hers, she might want it back, then we'd have no way . . . I'm sure it *was* the pendant that brought us here."

They walked through the hot green shadows of the wood almost without speaking again. Both were thinking their own thoughts, turning over the conversation they had just had with Emily Roman, thinking about her life; so different from their own.

"Playing the piano at dinner parties," Clare said. "Ugh! Emily probably spends a lot of time in the schoolroom. I never saw a schoolroom in a big house, like in books. I suppose we could go and look. No one would see us."

Richard nodded but didn't answer. He had liked Emily, in spite of her lapses into arrogance or pettishness. She wasn't stupid. There was honesty in her, though maybe deeply buried. She was a product of her times, yet there was something that seemed to want to break free. Aunt Ada might have had some influence.

"Maybe we can help her," Richard said finally. "Though I can't really work it out. After all, it's all happened already. So can we alter people's views and the things they do? Anyway, it's interesting; and it's funny how quickly we've gotten used to this adventure. We aren't scared anymore. We aren't even worrying if we'll get back home all right." Nevertheless, he found that he was holding his breath as they came to the stile and looked over the fields to the eastern side of the valley.

A combine harvester had moved into the field nearest their new home. It was painted bright blue and showed up clearly as it moved through the oats.

"So we're back," said Clare. "And, oh, Richard, all the lovely flowers will go! The poppies and marguerites and cornflowers. But listen, I've got an idea. We'll get our money tomorrow, Saturday, and I expect the village store sells film. We'll take some color prints of the village, and the new houses, and Romansgrove House; then we can show them to Emily."

"Gosh! That's a good idea!" her brother exclaimed.

"And we could take the camera with us next time and try to get some pictures of Emily and the Manor."

In the drawing room of Romansgrove Manor, Emily sat drinking tea with her mother. She usually had tea up in the schoolroom, of course, but now her mother was insisting on hearing her piece on the drawing room piano. And when she did, there would be trouble, for Emily hated the piece. She hated all stupid pieces, though she did like real music. Once—only once—she had been taken to a concert in London, and had heard a great and famous orchestra playing Beethoven. That had been marvelous.

Aunt Ada had taken her. Aunt Ada lived in London, *alone*. It must be terrible not to be married, but Aunt Ada didn't seem to mind. She lived in a little house in Mayfair and was on all kinds of committees. She was always addressing meetings; fighting for women's rights. Only one time had Emily ever been allowed to stay with her, even for one night. And that one time Aunt Ada had said: "I want you to hear real music, and I have two tickets for one of the best concerts of the season. I hate that terrible tinkling drawing room stuff. If you don't get some idea of what good music sounds like, your taste will be ruined forever. And you must see some good modern pictures, too."

Aunt Ada had had a near quarrel with Papa before permission was given, but she had retreated in triumph with her niece. They had gone to London by train, and then had come that wonderful music that echoed through Emily's head still. The next morning Aunt Ada had taken her to an exhibition of paintings by Cézanne, Utrillo, Marquet and Derain. They were not at all like the family portraits at Romansgrove Manor. Emily had started by being utterly bewildered, then had begun to *see*. It was as if a door had opened and she had walked through into a different world. Her discontent had really started at that time, six months earlier. Though even before that she had wanted to go to school.

She played the piano for her mother stumblingly, then was dismissed in disgrace to the schoolroom, where Miss Grace was doing some embroidery and was not inclined to be friendly.

So Emily at last allowed the memory of that strange meeting by the lake to come into the front of her mind. She remembered clearly all the things that Clare and Richard had said, and suddenly she seemed to be looking at her governess anew. Love! Maybe she really did love that curate with the prominent Adam's apple, and, if so, what did it feel like? Perhaps she, Emily, *had* been unkind . . . had really blackmailed her. Blackmail . . . that was an awful word.

As the sky darkened, threatening thunder, Emily went meekly to her bedroom to wash before schoolroom supper. Lizzie Moult, the schoolroom maid (she was a cousin of Jenny and Tim), came toiling up the stairs from the kitchen with hot water in a pitcher. Lizzie was sixteen and had started as kitchen maid, like Jenny. She hated being schoolroom maid, though she had learned long ago to hide her feelings. All those stairs and never a word of thanks. Even that Grace Matthews thought herself too good to speak to a mere schoolroom maid;

except, of course, when she wanted something.

So Lizzie nearly jumped out of her skin when Emily actually smiled at her and said: "Thank you, Lizzie."

Lizzie stared at her young mistress, ready to bolt.

"Did Jenny get back, Lizzie? She went to see her mother, I believe."

"Oh, Jenny, Miss . . . Yes, Miss. She were late. Cook was annoyed."

"Tell Mrs. Brewer it was my fault. I sent her for a shawl and that delayed her."

"Yes, Miss. No, Miss. Thank you, Miss." And Lizzie fled with the empty pitcher. She all but fell down the narrow back stairs, so eager was she to confound Cook with Emily's message. Like all the other young girls, she hated Mrs. Brewer. One thing about being school-room maid was that it did get her out of the kitchen sometimes. As it was, she spent quite enough of her long working day helping Ellen and Jenny under the cook's ill-tempered supervision.

"I'll just get myself married soon as I can," she muttered to herself, as she pushed open the kitchen door.

Emily slowly washed her face in the rose-patterned basin. They were human. They had rights. *Rights.* Of course she must have imagined that girl and boy. Clare and Richard Manley. *Could* she have imagined their names? And all that talk about bathrooms in cottages, and central heating. She only used the bathroom once a week, when she took her bath, and of course to go to the water closet. But even that wasn't expected in the night, or if she was in a hurry. There was a rose-patterned chamber pot under her bed, and it was part of Lizzie's work to empty it. For the very first time Emily wondered if Lizzie minded that.

Emily dried her hands and then gave her red ringlets a twist here and there. She was thinking of a girl wearing an old green blouse and blue trousers with narrow legs. Shocking! But a girl with a pretty, friendly face, who seemed on very good terms with her brother. Never once had Richard said, "You're only a girl!" and laughed at her, as Alan did constantly when he came to visit.

They had said that women had the vote, and Richard had seemed to think they had had it for a long time. Politics, Emily had always thought, were boring and only for men. Yet Aunt Ada . . . Emily's father had said she was either mad or years ahead of her time, but in his opinion she ought to be put away some place where she couldn't disgrace the family and get herself into real trouble.

For the very first time Emily Roman surveyed herself in the mirror in her pretty bedroom and saw herself fighting for something, like Aunt Ada. Those gypsies hadn't thought much of her, and that hurt her pride. She usually had a very good opinion of herself. Gypsies or ghosts from the future? Emily shivered as a sudden flash of lightning showed up the freckles on her nose. Ghosts, nonsense! It was a joke, or a trick. But she found that she very much wanted to see them again.

7

THE
OLD DRIVEWAY

Clare and Richard's "summer secret" was not wholly hidden. Their father was much absorbed in his new job; he was interested in learning more about the running of the estate, and, being the man he was, was constantly on the lookout for something to criticize. He found very few things of which to disapprove, beyond the fact of its being an inherited estate, but his mind was constantly occupied. However, Mrs. Manley had time on her hands so far, and she was obviously puzzled by her son and daughter.

"Did you meet anyone?" she asked after supper, when the expected storm was raging over the valley.

Clare and Richard looked at each other.

"Well, one or two people, Mother," said Clare.

"You'll have to start making some friends. I believe there are children at North Farm, and two boys at East Farm."

"Why not ask them to tea or something?" asked Mr. Manley, looking up from the local evening paper, which he had picked up in the village.

"That's an idea. And Victoria Roman will be back soon, I understand. She's Clare's age."

"Victoria will have her own friends. I suppose she goes to some posh boarding school," Clare remarked.

"Shouldn't be boarding schools," Mr. Manley muttered into his newspaper. "No private schools at all. Only state education."

He was so much more his old self that Clare dared to laugh.

"All countries have boarding schools, don't they, Dad? Even in America. It might be fun to go to one. Sleeping in dormitories, and having midnight feasts, the way they did in old stories."

"Lot of rubbish!" he said, quite cheerfully, and went on reading.

On Saturday morning Clare and Richard were given their pocket money for the next week. They went off to the village in search of chocolate and a film for Clare's camera. It was no use trying to escape to Roman's Grove. Lunch was to be very early, then they were going out in the car. "To explore the countryside," their father had said. "We'll take a walk on the hills."

Clare took her camera to the village, so, when the film had been bought and put in, she began to think about pictures. It was cooler after the storm, but still sunny. In fact, the light was perfect for photographs. She took a few, and Richard took others. They planned it carefully, taking shots that might convince Emily Roman. Well-dressed, healthy village children playing by the duck pond, some of the new houses, the estate office, where the affairs of Romansgrove were dealt with, and—on the way home—the combine harvester in the field opposite their house.

"Next time we climb the slope we'll take one across the valley," said Richard. "Of Romansgrove House on the hill."

Though it was a pleasant day, both felt frustrated that they had not been able to go back and meet Emily. Perhaps she had been waiting for them, sitting in the blue boat on the lake.

"We'll go tomorrow morning," said Richard, when they took a stroll up the valley after supper. They had not been that way yet, following the road to North Farm and on over the hills. The road was narrow, so narrow that there were passing places here and there, but there was little traffic to trouble them.

They had left the entrance to North Farm two or three hundred yards behind them when Clare suddenly turned to the left. She had a bemused air, and Richard looked at her in surprise.

"Where are you going?"

"To the Manor," she said. "This is the driveway."

And then she stopped, faced with an overgrown tangle of bushes and briars. The bemused look left her face, and she stared in surprise. "Rich, I really thought for a moment . . . and there *is* a footpath, I think. Only it's terribly overgrown."

Richard searched around in the high bracken on either side, and suddenly he pushed the bracken down and exposed a broad stone stump. Half visible in the undergrowth was more stone, lying against the earth. He moved to the other side and saw exactly the same. Once there had been gateposts there, sufficiently far apart to take a carriage and pair.

"But how did you *know?*" he asked.

"Because I've been," Clare said. "Don't you remember the driveway?"

Richard shook his head. "No, I've never been here before. You know I haven't."

"But I *have*. Maybe it's stronger for me, because I found the pendant. I expect you were there, too. This was the old way to the Manor. I'm sure of that."

"But look, Clare, you *haven't* been here before! We went each time through Roman's Grove, and back the same way. You *know*.

Clare frowned, pushing her hair out of her eyes.

"Yes, I do know that. But some time I was on this drive. There were church bells in the distance."

For a moment Richard looked at his sister with something like awe. She stood in the bracken, with one foot on a broken gatepost. Her thin arms were already suntanned, and her yellow cotton dress was blowing in the gusty wind. Of course, he had been to the house; he had seen it and the top of the driveway, but this was something different. The mysteries of time made him afraid.

"Well," he said, after a few moments, "the old drive had to come out somewhere, and these *were* gateposts. If it wound a little, and climbed, it would go in the direction of the Manor. But we're not going to try to explore what's left of it tonight. Besides, though there does seem to be a kind of path, it's terribly overgrown. I don't believe we'd get through. It might be different in winter."

"What we need is a map," Clare said, as they went on up the present-day road. "An old map, I mean. Perhaps there's one in the library at Painsden. Even a new map would be a help. It would show footpaths and the ruined Manor."

"Yes, that's right. We'll try to find something when we go to Painsden."

There seemed to be nothing up the road but the tree-crowned northern ridge, so, since it was getting late, they turned and retraced their steps.

"Do you know," said Clare, "I've been wondering all day what Emily has been doing. I know it's silly, but I can't help wanting tomorrow to come in a hurry so she can tell us. Around now she may be playing her 'piece' in the drawing room. Or maybe they have a music room at the Manor."

They were both quiet then, wondering together at the ease with which they spoke. It was more than seventy years since Emily had played her piece, but perhaps she was playing it still, in that frozen moment of time. If time were a continuing ribbon, there she was, surrounded by dinner guests. Was it really possible that it was so?

"Let's run." Richard said. "It's downhill all the way, and the wind will be more or less behind us."

They ran as fast as they could, laughing, racing. It was a relief to shake off, even for a short while, the vivid memories.

The Manleys rarely stayed in bed late on Sunday mornings, and that Sunday was fine and still, with the chilly wind that had followed the storm completely gone. Breakfast was over by nine o'clock, and forty-five minutes later the beds were made, the dishes washed, and vegetables prepared for lunch. Mrs. Manley said she wanted to do a little gardening, and Mr. Manley sat reading the Sunday newspaper that had been delivered by Tom Moult.

"Lunch at one o'clock," Mrs. Manley told Clare and Richard, as they prepared to set off. "You two are in an awful hurry. Where are you going?"

"We're still exploring, Mother," Clare said quickly, guiltily. "And we do love Roman's Grove."

The green path lay clearly between the acres of pale gold stubble, and Clare missed the flowers that had grown on the edge of the ripe oats. But the next field was still uncut, and the silky barley hemmed them in, as high as their shoulders. It made faintly moving, shimmering walls on either side.

They went as quickly as they could, but once they reached the depths of the wood, it was difficult to hurry. The way was clearer now, with their constant passing, but there were still roots to be avoided and obstinate brambles to disentangle from their clothes. That morning Clare wore her almost new jeans; they were dark tan, and her blouse was bright yellow. Clare always liked to have a pocket, and the pendant lay safely against her chest. She had worn her better clothes with some vague feeling that Emily would expect a difference on Sundays.

Richard glanced at her once or twice, and she laughed.

"You're wearing lipstick," he said.

"Well, why not? I'm old enough. Some girls of nearly fourteen are out with boys every evening. You know what it was like in town." And she sighed suddenly, remembering their last few months in the city. There had been a boy of fifteen she had rather liked, but it had all been forgotten in the strain and misery of family troubles. There had been one evening in the winter when the boy had taken her out for coffee and a sandwich, then to a movie, and her father had been angry when she came home late. "No daughter of mine at the age of thirteen . . ."

It all seemed long ago and in another life. Now they were in the heart of this strange country, and there were no boys, only Richard. Though Richard was a wonderful companion.

"Yes, I know," said her brother. "But why now, to go to the Manor?"

Clare shrugged and laughed again.

"I don't know. I saw the lipstick and I wondered what Emily would say. She seems so real, but we're worlds apart."

Fifty minutes had passed before they neared the end of the wood. That was the quickest they had done the journey from South Lodge, though going back the last time it had taken only forty minutes. The last mile across the valley was nearly all downhill.

It was always a strange, suspenseful moment when they came out from the trees, but the Manor was there, peaceful and golden. The peacocks strutted on the terraces, although there was no person in sight. The blue boat was empty. Clare, who had her camera slung over her shoulder in its case, stopped and took a picture.

"Of course she may have to read the Bible or something on Sundays," Clare whispered, as they walked boldly across the short grass and began to climb the shallow steps. "By their time it's not ten o'clock yet. They'll go to church, won't they? I'd forgotten that."

On the first terrace Clare paused to run her hands over the sun-warmed stone of a statue . . . a classical maiden in carved draperies. The very same broken statue she has stumbled over the day they'd found the Manor in ruins.

They felt perfectly safe, for only Emily could see them. She might even be looking for them. Clare's eyes searched the windows of the big house. The main bedrooms would look this way, surely, over the grass, the lake and the woods? The kitchen wing was at the back, they knew, but where was the schoolroom? There were three stories, with a few small, higher windows in the gables.

"Do you think we dare go in?" she asked.

Before Richard could reply, there was a sudden violent barking, and the white terrier they had seen the first time shot out from behind a low box hedge. He danced around their feet, yapping and showing his teeth. Clare was so startled that she stepped back and almost fell into the low basin of a fountain.

"He can see us!" she gasped, righting herself just in time. "Oh, Rich! What shall we do?"

"Well, he can sense us, anyway," said Richard, side-stepping. The dog immediately followed him, still barking.

"Oh, good boy! Good dog! Here, do make friends," Clare pleaded. "We like you. We're not enemies or burglars. Friends of your mistress. Where's Emily?"

Could the dog hear? At the sound of the name, he stopped barking and eyed them in a less belligerent way. Then he started again. The sound echoed over the sunlit scene, breaking the total peace of Sunday morning.

Someone had heard . . . there was a figure standing at an open French window on the terrace above them. A maid, wearing a long print dress, a white apron and an elaborate white cap. A fretful voice came from behind her. Lady Roman's voice.

"Such a noise! Where is Miss Emily, Maggie? Find her and make her take the wretched animal indoors. I must get ready for church. It's nearly ten o'clock. When you find Miss Emily, and the dog is shut up, tell her I wish to see her at *once*."

And then Emily herself came around the west side of the house . . . the side away from the main door. She took in the scene at a glance and came running along the top terrace, leaping the steps to the next one. She snatched the dog up in her arms, at the same time saying in a low voice:

"I heard him barking. So it seems you are real, after all. I've wanted to see you again, but now there will be trouble."

"No, there won't," Richard said quickly. "It's only the dog. But your mother wants to speak to you. Look! There's a maid, and your mother's in the room behind her."

Emily whirled as the maid said: "Miss Emily, her Ladyship wants to speak to you."

"Oh, how tiresome!" Emily started up the steps. The maid disappeared and Emily followed her through the French window. Clare and Richard followed, shrinking a little, but sure it was safe to go close.

They did not go into the room. There was no need, and, as Clare said later, they might have knocked something over. It was a big room, but it was crowded with heavy, ornate furniture and many whatnots and low tables, each covered with objects: vases, china figurines, carved boxes.

Lady Roman, hatless and wearing a long dark green dress, was standing a few feet within the room. Her flaming hair was elaborately arranged, and she was a very handsome woman, or would have been if she hadn't been so pale and bad-tempered looking.

"That was a *disgraceful* noise on a Sunday morning, Emily," she said. "When we allowed you to have the dog, you promised to look after him and keep him under control. You know I don't like dogs. Take him to the schoolroom, and then you and Miss Grace are to get ready as quickly as possible. You are to walk to church. That is to be your punishment for your dreadful performance at my dinner party last night. And to lose your temper . . . to shame me by your bad manners, as well as by your bad playing. Your father says that perhaps for once your Aunt Ada is right and you need more exercise. You are too much for me, and I have no wish to drive down to church with you. If you behave well during the service, you will be allowed to drive back. I have already told Miss Grace. I hope she will be nearly ready."

Emily stood with the dog in her arms. She wore a stiff white dress, with elaborate embroidery, and the broad sash was also white, tied in a big bow behind.

"It's no punishment to walk to church, Mama. And Miss Grace also likes walking."

"It should be a punishment to arrive on foot, like the servants and the village people. Do go and lock up that dog. You will make your dress dirty and that will add to your disgrace."

"Rex is clean. I bathed him yesterday morning," said Emily.

"You should have asked that boy, Tim Moult, to do it. That is one of his duties, and by what your father heard, he is idle enough in the stable yard."

"I like washing Rex, Mama. And *I* am tired of being idle."

"Then you should work harder at your lessons and piano practice."

"But it's summer. I shouldn't do lessons now. Girls are home from boarding school and . . ."

"Oh, go!"

Emily cast one glance over her shoulder. She winked deliberately at Clare and Richard, standing out on the terrace, and then whirled away through the door into the passage. If Emily had ever been afraid of ghosts, she wasn't now. And she knew very well that her mother couldn't see Clare and Richard, though they were so close to the French window.

"So what do we do now?" Clare whispered. She knew she couldn't be heard, yet it still seemed necessary to speak quietly.

"Go to church with them," her brother murmured back. "We can walk down behind Emily and Miss Grace . . . see what happens."

"You mean we may see Romansgrove village then? Would it work?"

"It might. Let's try. We'll wait by the front door."

They walked around the house and were startled to see that the carriage was already waiting at the front door. It really was a very splendid vehicle, drawn by two shining chestnuts. The coachman, who was the man who had driven the trap the first time, was lounging on the box, with the air of being ready to wait all day. Perhaps Sir Alan Roman insisted that everyone be early.

In not much more than five minutes Emily emerged from the porch, ahead of Miss Grace. Emily now wore a big white hat, with blue ribbons, white gloves and beautiful little white boots. In her right hand she carried a prayer book, and hanging from her other wrist was a small white bag with a draw string.

Her face crinkled into laughter when she saw Clare

and Richard, but the coachman was watching. Without speaking she flicked her long reddish lashes and started off. Miss Grace, wearing a light brown dress and a dowdy hat to match, had to hurry to catch up with her.

Clare and Richard fell in behind. The drive curved, as they already knew, leaving the great entrance to the stable yard on their left. There were dark rhododendrons and laurels for some distance, then the road went downhill between fields. As the view opened out, they could see, ahead of Emily and Miss Grace, a straggling group of people in dark clothes. The servants, too, were on their way to divine service.

On their right, from the village, came the sound of church bells.

"There you are!" Clare whispered triumphantly. "I told you I'd been here before. Hear the bells?"

"But you *hadn't!* You're here now, but . . ."

Clare gave a baffled look and shook her head.

In front of them Emily said clearly: "Miss Grace, have you ever seen a girl around my age wearing trousers and with painted lips?"

There was a shocked silence, then Miss Grace asked: "Emily have you taken leave of your senses?"

"Maybe I have," answered Emily, and giggled. "Miss Grace, tell me this, then. Do you believe in ghosts?"

"What a very strange question. You really are not quite yourself this morning. No, of course I don't believe in ghosts."

"Or people from the past or future?"

"People can't come from the past or future. You know that quite well."

"But there are stories. Strange things that have happened."

"Just the stupid superstitions of village folk."

"Perhaps village folk are not quite so stupid as I have always thought."

"They are uneducated, Emily. No one expects much of them."

"Maybe they should be educated."

"The young ones go to the school in the village. It's right that they should work as soon as they can."

"Should *I* work as soon as I can?" Emily cast one flickering glance over her shoulder.

"Don't be absurd, child!" Miss Grace sounded irritated. "Girls of your station in life don't work. You'll be presented at Court and make a suitable marriage."

"It doesn't sound very exciting, except that I'd like to see King Edward and Queen Alexandra. *You* work, Miss Grace, though I don't think you like it very much."

"I had no choice," the governess said. "My father is a poor clergyman, as you know, and there are ten of us."

"It doesn't seem very sensible to have ten children when . . ." Then Emily stopped, aware that she had said something outrageous. "I'm sorry, Miss Grace. Of course God means people to have children when they are married. But I once heard Aunt Ada say . . ."

"Emily!" Miss Grace sounded tried almost beyond endurance, and also deeply shocked. "Say no more, I beg of you. We will walk in silence."

Clare and Richard had listened entranced to the conversation.

"She's coming on," Clare said. "Really starting to

think." And Emily's shoulders moved, the little white bag swung in a small arc, but she did not look around.

Clare had stopped briefly to take a photograph of the downward stretch of the driveway, and she took one more as the first group of servants approached the great open gates.

"I wonder if these pictures will come out?" she said, in a low voice. "I think I got it all in. Miss Grace and Emily, and all the servants way ahead, and that pretty little lodge."

As Miss Grace and Emily approached the gates, an old woman came out of the lodge. She wore a shabby print dress and a faded pink sunbonnet. She curtsied briefly, but did not smile. Her pale blue eyes were alight with curiosity.

"Good morning, Miss Emily. Good morning, Miss." Clearly she could hardly believe that she was seeing Miss Emily Roman on foot on a Sunday morning, close on the heels of the Manor servants.

Emily offered no explanation.

"The carriage and the trap will be down in a few minutes," was all she said.

"Is everything all right, Miss Emily?"

"Of course, Martha. Thank you." And Emily and the governess passed through the gates and turned to the right into the narrow road.

The old woman retreated to her rose-hung front door, muttering to herself: "First time I ever heard *her* say thank you."

Clare and Richard paused to look at the gates. They were high, splendidly wrought and painted in black and gold. The posts were topped with carved heads . . . the same ones that were on the gates beside South Lodge in modern times.

Emily and Miss Grace were walking pretty fast, and Clare and Richard hurried to catch up with them. They passed the entrance to North Farm (a little different, but recognizable) and continued rapidly down the valley. They had just drawn level with the place where South Lodge was later to be built when the sound of horse's hooves made them all draw to one side. It was a pony and trap, and in it were a red-faced farmer, a fat woman in a bonnet, and three small children. The man looked astonished and stopped the pony.

"Miss Emily, is something the matter? The carriage?"

"Nothing's the matter, Soames, thank you," said Emily, with dignity. "Miss Grace and I wished to walk this morning."

"Yes, Miss. All right, Miss." And the farmer drove on.

"Really the Soames family are quite nice," said Emily to Miss Grace. "Soames works hard at North Farm. But you know my father is most annoyed with him. The farmhouse, according to Soames, is in a bad state. Not fit for keeping cattle in, he told Papa. Papa was very angry. The cattle, in fact, have new buildings. Cattle are valuable. Do you think that's right, Miss Grace? Do you think all people should have bathrooms?"

"I told you to be quiet, Emily," Miss Grace said sharply. "We have had enough of your Aunt Ada's ideas for one morning."

At that moment another trap approached and passed them. It was one from the Manor, driven by the man who had beaten Tim Moult. With him was the cook, Mrs. Brewer, looking larger than ever in Sunday clothes of sober gray, an elderly woman in black and the man they had seen briefly on their first visit and assumed was the butler.

"The one in black must be the housekeeper," Richard remarked, and, ahead of them, Emily's head nodded. "At least Sir Alan doesn't make *them* walk."

"Mrs. Brewer would never get to church at all if she had to walk," said Emily, and giggled. Miss Grace took no notice of her, merely walked faster. It was very hard on Emily that she could not speak directly to her new friends.

Then, as they approached the village, in the loud clangor of the bells, the carriage from the Manor overtook them, bearing Sir Alan Roman and his wife to church. There were no new houses now, only the old cottages and the inn around the village green. The store was a cottage with two bowfront windows.

Outside the church the village people waited. As the young people and Miss Grace approached the lych-gate, Sir Alan and Lady Roman were walking past the curtsying tenants. This was the year 1902, in a remote part of England, and the future was almost undreamed of, even though young Emily Roman had started to ask questions.

8

THE
FAMILY PEW

The church was dim and cool, with small, rounded windows on the one side, filled with plain glass. The other side, the south, was much more ornate, and there was a good deal of dark stained glass in the intricate pattern of the windows.

"A bit of Norman work on one side, and Perpendicular on the other," Richard said to himself. They had been learning about architecture in school. "And some of that colored glass is fairly new. Late Victorian, I should think. A memorial window to one of the Romans." For he had glimpsed the same heads that were on the gateposts, and the word ROMAN.

But he had little time for thinking. He and Clare had

stuck as close to Miss Grace and Emily as possible, and *they* were behind Sir Alan and Lady Roman. Most of the pews were black with age, and the Manor pew, down near the chancel and placed sideways, had high wooden sides and a door. A real, ancient box pew. Someone was playing the organ, and the bells overhead sounded a last violent peal before changing to a final warning bell.

Clare whispered urgently into Richard's ear: "Don't let's go into their pew! There may not be room, and we'd never get out if we wanted to."

"We haven't tried walking through doors," her brother murmured back, and she said, "What?", then realized what he had said and smiled.

A man who seemed to be a church warden was deferentially showing the Romans and Miss Grace into the pew. Clare and Richard stood to one side, in a space near the pulpit. The musty, cool smell was so real, the whole scene so pulsing with quiet life, that they both felt conspicuous, sure that someone would cry out: "Who are these strange children?" But no one did. They were invisible to all but Emily.

The Manor servants had filed into several short pews on the opposite side of the chancel, with the older and more important ones in the front row. Mrs. Brewer's gray outfit was hideous. Her red, fat face was framed in a huge bonnet, and she looked as ill-tempered now as she had when she was shouting at Jenny Moult. Not a pleasant woman, and not one who looked ready and willing to take part in divine service. But Sir Alan expected it of his staff . . . cold lunch on Sundays.

On the outside of the front pew—the place of honor?

—sat the housekeeper. She was a tall, serious-looking woman, very thin and quite elderly. She looked stiff and without humor, but it must be a great responsibility to be in charge of household matters at Romansgrove Manor.

"Do you think she—that housekeeper one—once started as kitchen maid?" Clare whispered. "Oh, Rich, isn't it *fascinating?*"

The butler, the coachman and a drab, pale-faced woman, who might be the head housemaid, also sat in the front row. Behind them were several young women and girls, probably all housemaids, but not Maggie, who had called to Emily on the terrace. *Someone* must have to stay home. Some must go to evening service instead. The cruel man who had beaten Tim Moult and Tim Moult himself were near the back, with other men, un-easy in Sunday clothes. Gardeners, perhaps. At first Clare couldn't see Jenny Moult, then she spied her in a dark corner, under a heavy Victorian memorial. She was dabbing her nose with a rag, as if she had been cry-ing or had a cold, and she wore a broken straw hat.

The rest of the church was filled with cottage women, farmers and their wives, and estate workers. There were a lot of old women, very shabby and with faces so worn that they might have been a hundred years old. And there were a great many children, poorly dressed and undernourished. Some sat with their parents, and others were together in a group, with a pretty, nervous-looking young woman. A Sunday school class, perhaps.

The service had started while they were staring, and

the Vicar was announcing the first hymn. He was an old man, thin and tired looking. And there was another man in a surplice . . . he was quite young and looked as if he didn't have enough to eat. He kept blinking nervously, and his prominent Adam's apple wobbled as he sang.

"Do you think that's Mr. Baines?" Clare asked. "If it is, *I* don't know why Miss Grace is in love with him. He isn't at all handsome."

It was all very strange to Clare and Richard, but it would have been almost as strange to them if they had been attending a service in the same church in modern times. Once they had been taken to a cathedral with other members of their class, but otherwise they had never been to church. Neither their father nor their mother went, and saw no reason for their children to do so.

The hymn ended, everyone sat down noisily, and Sir Alan Roman left the family pew to read the first lesson. Clare and Richard, with one accord, looked at Emily, and Emily was staring straight at them, obviously trying hard not to smile. It would be rather fun, but mean, to make Emily laugh. She and Miss Grace would have to walk home to the Manor if she disgraced herself in church.

A second hymn . . . sung with gusto by everyone. It was called "All Things Bright and Beautiful." Richard listened in amazement.

> *The rich man in his castle,*
> *The poor man at his gate,*

the rich man in his castle

III

God made them high or lowly,
And ordered their estate.

And everyone was singing it as if it was quite natural that God might have planned that Tim Moult should be beaten and probably slept in the straw, and that Lady Roman should live in the utmost luxury, with servants to answer her every whim. As if it were right that village children should be nearly in rags, while Miss Emily Roman was dressed in stiff muslin, with beautiful white boots on her feet.

"Let's go!" Richard said, as the hymn seemed to be drawing to a close.

"Oh, not yet! I don't want to miss anything," Clare pleaded.

But her brother was already making his way up the center aisle. Faces swam at her as she followed; worn faces under awful bonnets or battered hats. The tile floor was slippery. Turning to the left toward the door, Clare skidded in her nervous hurry not to be left behind. Lurching, she clutched at a stand loaded with extra hymnbooks, and the stand fell over with a crash, scattering hymnbooks in all directions. Clare fled after Richard (luckily, on such a fine morning, the door was open), but not before she had heard, in the silence that followed the end of the hymn, Emily Roman give a high, hysterical giggle.

Richard had paused in the porch and was staring back into the church.

"What on earth happened?" he asked. "All those books . . ."

Clare, gasping and pink-faced with suppressed mirth and horror, clutched his arm.

"I did it. I slipped. *We* may be invisible, Rich, but the books aren't. And the *crash* . . . just at the end of the hymn!"

The violent cascade of hymnbooks, apparently for no reason, had certainly interrupted the service. The two lingering in the porch saw the church warden come hurrying up the aisle, and the village people had turned around in their seats.

But the Vicar, choosing to ignore the episode, was making his way to the pulpit for the sermon.

"And I bet it lasts an hour," said Richard. "You were a clumsy fool to do that. Was it Emily who laughed?"

"Yes, and I don't blame her. Who would have thought a ghost from the future would have any substance?" Clare remarked. "But I felt the hymnbooks and they felt me. I'm going to have a bruise on my arm."

"Emily's going to be in trouble, you know."

Clare looked sober at once.

"I'm sorry about that, when she was in trouble already. I didn't *intend* to make her laugh, though I thought of it earlier and decided it would be mean."

"So did I," Richard agreed. "Well, there's nothing we can do. We can't tell her mother it was our fault, and Emily can't tell her she saw a ghost slip and knock down the hymnbooks. They would only say she was telling lies and lock her in the schoolroom or something. Let's go and see the village. We only had a glimpse on the way to church."

They walked down the path between the great old

yew trees, and through the lych-gate. At first sight the village was charming; there seemed to be nothing to spoil the idyllic scene. No scarlet telephone booth, no traffic signs, no television aerials and advertisements. The cottages dreamed under showers of small yellow roses, and the little store with its bow windows looked delightful. Clare pressed her nose against the right-hand window and exclaimed over the old-fashioned candies, the little dolls costing one penny and tiny models of coaches and carts, also only a penny.

The glass in the door looked very old, thick in places, so that everything was a trifle distorted, but they could see into the store.

"Such a lovely jumble!" cried Clare. "Everyone must be able to get what they want here. Look, Rich! Old lamps and tools and food all mixed together. Much more fun than the way it is now—in our time, I mean—with plate-glass windows and a refrigerator crammed with frozen fish and hamburgers."

"It doesn't look very clean, though," said Richard. "Sawdust on the floor, and it looks pretty dirty. And there are flies crawling on that bacon."

They turned away and continued with their survey of old Romansgrove village. Instead of parked cars and trucks there were a few traps, the horses tied to posts. A young boy, very raggedly dressed, was keeping guard over the Romans' carriage and pair. As they watched, he skipped across the green to the inn, and came back two minutes latter with what looked like a hunk of bread and cheese. He tried to hide himself behind the horses and ate the food with a guilty air.

"He's probably the stable lad at the inn," said Richard. "But they evidently don't treat him badly there. He got that bread pretty quickly."

Clare quickly took a picture and then wound the roll off.

"That's the last," she said regretfully. "But I think I got some of the cottages in, as well as the coach and horses and the boy. I *wonder* if they'll come out?"

The cottages were very old and very pretty, but second glances showed broken roof tiles, sagging gutterings and a general air of disrepair. On a summer morning their charm predominated, but on a winter's day it must be very different.

In the doorway of a cottage near the store, a very old woman sat in a rocking chair, muttering to herself. On the little front path of another house three small barefoot children were playing with stones. The children were filthy, and one had a sore close to her mouth. Another, a boy of about three, had a bad case of ringworm; his hair had been cut away to show his scalp.

"If father could see this . . ." Richard muttered.

"But this is long before Father was a boy. Forty years or more."

"I know. But remember his stories. Things hadn't improved much in that Cheshire village."

"They must have. People didn't curtsy anymore, and I don't suppose most of them went to church," Clare protested.

"People were still poor. Of course it was wartime when Father was a boy. He says it was the war that made things better, in the end. People wanted something better. And then the Health Service was started, and kids began having free milk and orange juice, so they were healthier." Richard frowned at the happy ducks on the village pond. "Just think what we could tell Emily. A million, million things. Planes flying all over the world every minute of the day and night. Television . . . radar . . . even radio. They didn't have that. And even ordinary workers taking it for granted they must have a car, and a washing machine, and a refrigerator. Is that the village pump? I suppose that's all they have for water."

Clare worked the pump handle experimentally. A stream of water gushed out, and she jumped back. The boy by the carriage and pair was staring across the green, his mouth open in astonishment. "Ghosts!" said Clare. "He saw it work by itself."

"And Emily doesn't know about real warfare, or the atom bomb, or . . ." Richard went on.

"We mustn't scare the poor girl. We're used to it. I should think Women's Lib would interest her more. She sure needs that."

"She isn't scared of *us* now, anyway," Richard remarked. "She isn't a bad kind of girl, or she wouldn't be if she had a chance. Clare, how are we going to get back?"

Clare jumped. They were heading away from the village now, past the place where the estate office was later to be, surrounded by new houses.

"I don't know," she confessed. "I'd forgotten the strangeness of our being here. It's all been so interesting. Shall we go back to the wood?"

The lane was narrower than in modern times; the banks were high and thickly overgrown with flowers and ferns. They felt that there was no danger from traffic, and they walked in the middle of the road.

It was a violent shock then when there was a loud hooting sound and something seemed to swish at them. Richard yelled and dragged Clare aside. Utterly dazed, they found themselves looking into the face of the modern Lord Romansgrove, as he looked out of the driver's window of a big car.

"Want to get yourselves killed, you two?" he asked. "Right on a bend . . . you did give me a scare! Are you all right?"

Maybe he thought their dazed state understandable. He didn't seem to find it excessive.

"Oh, yes, we're all right. We're sorry," Richard said.

Lady Romansgrove was beside her husband, and there were three people in the back of the big car. Richard's gaze, and Clare's, fastened on the brilliant red hair of a young girl, who was staring through the open window beside the back seat.

"Emily!" Clare cried involuntarily, but Lord Romansgrove's voice cut across the name. "We've been to meet Victoria off the morning train. Not many trains on Sundays. You'll meet her later. And do watch out, you two. These roads are too narrow for modern traffic."

The big car went on, and Clare and Richard stood staring at each other. The road might be narrow, but it was no longer such a winding lane, and there, ahead, were the gates of Romansgrove House, and the car was turning in.

"But it was Emily!" Clare cried. "Emily, with her red hair gone straight. I'd know that nose anywhere, and it even had freckles on it. Emily in a car, and wearing . . . What was she wearing? A sleeveless sweater, I think . . . blue. Richard, it was so quick! We're back, of course."

"Yes, and that wasn't Emily. It was Victoria Roman," her brother pointed out. "We might have been killed, wandering in the middle of the road like that. But we were thinking in terms of horses and traps, and they were all waiting outside the church. There were two other people in the back of the car with Victoria."

"Yes, I saw, but I was so muddled . . . Old ladies. Her grandmother, perhaps, and a friend or an aunt. I didn't see them clearly. It's so disconcerting to be there one moment and here the next."

It was 12:45 as they approached South Lodge. Mrs. Manley was in the garden, grubbing around on her hands and knees. She looked up when she heard them.

"Oh, here you are! Your father has gone to see the man at North Farm, a Mr. Soames. Apparently he was in the estate office on Friday and was talking about his wonderful new milking machine and other improvements. The beef's in the oven, and the vegetables are cooking. What's the matter?"

"We . . . we were walking in the road and the Romans' car came rather quickly," said Clare. "We had a fright."

"You really will have to be careful. Yes, I saw the car. That must be Victoria home again. What's the matter with your arm, Clare? That's a nasty mark."

"I . . . I must have bumped it," Clare mumbled. Far

away, in the past, she had nearly fallen and knocked down several dozen hymnbooks. The sermon was probably still going on now. It was very confusing.

"Thank heaven for first-aid boxes!" Mrs. Manley said gaily. She wiped her hands together and led the way indoors.

Mr. Manley arrived back ten minutes later. During the meal Richard said to his father: "Dad, did you go to church when you were a boy?"

Mr. Manley looked at his son in a startled way.

"Well, yes, sometimes. Until I was around twelve. Or maybe thirteen. I sang in the choir."

"Was there a hymn called 'All Things Bright and Beautiful'?"

Mr. Manley's face took on a different expression.

"Yes, there was. I hated it. 'The rich man in his castle, The poor man at his gate . . .' I expect they still sing it, but someone once told me that particular verse had been cut out. Why?"

"I just wondered," Richard said, and fortunately Clare knocked over her glass of water at that moment. So there were no more questions.

9

AUNT ADA

It was difficult to think of anything but their recent experiences. That other world now seemed as real as the one in which they customarily moved and spoke and ate.

"But we mustn't let it get too great a hold on us," Clare said later, a little scared. "It's strange how quickly we've grown used to the idea of going back. But say there came a point when we couldn't return here?"

"I don't think that's a danger," Richard said. "At least not yet."

"Maybe it's some kind of illusion, after all," Clare murmured. They lay on cushions on the little lawn, each with a book, but the printed word could not hold them at the moment.

"Sometimes I wonder," he agreed. "But it seems so real. I keep on trying to imagine how Emily got on after church."

Clare stirred restlessly. "Could we go now?"

"I don't think so. Mother said she might come for a walk with us later. We could take her to Roman's Grove and show her the remains of the Roman villa."

This they did, and Mrs. Manley was impressed by the green luminosity of the great wood . . . the wonderful old trees . . . and the small piece of tesselated flooring.

"How far is it to the end of the wood?" she asked, as she rose from her knees.

"Oh, quite a way yet." It was strange to be in the grove with their mother; nice to show it to her, but much of the magic seemed gone. In a way Clare felt bereft. She added, after a moment: "There's a ruined house."

"Oh, have you seen it? Someone mentioned it to me . . . in the bus on Friday, I think it was. The old Manor, wasn't it? I hope it isn't dangerous? Did you go inside?"

"No," said Richard, truthfully enough. "Some of the walls are high, and I suppose they *could* fall. I think the house was burned."

"Yes, I believe so, a long time ago. That's when the Romans built the new house on the opposite slope."

"Who told you?" Richard asked, trying to conceal his eagerness. She frowned, pushing her hair out of her eyes.

"A Mrs. Moult, I think. I met so many people that day. Yes, she said something about her son Tom going there with his dog. She said a strange thing. She said it was a good thing the house burned. Everyone hated the Romans then. They were bad landlords and too proud. It was only after that, that things began to get better."

"But how did she know? Tom Moult's only a kid. We met him. His mother can't be very old."

"She isn't as old as I am," Mrs. Manley agreed. "I've no idea how she knows. I suppose country people have long memories, especially for grievances. Your father would say all workers remember their past troubles . . . a kind of folk memory, if nothing else. But most people here seem happy now, and the Romans are certainly popular."

She did not seem to want to see the ruined house, so they returned by way of the path that went to the end of the ridge, then they strolled through the fields to South Farm and turned toward home through the village. The church bells were ringing for evening service, but there were not many people making their way toward the lych-gate. There were men outside the inn, sitting on two long benches.

"Waiting for opening time," said Mrs. Manley. "Seven o'clock on a Sunday."

"I wonder if the Romans go to church?" said Richard.

"I suppose they do sometimes. There probably won't be more than a dozen people at the service," his mother said casually.

Clare thought of the crowded church of 1902 . . . the worn faces and shabby clothes of the villagers and estate workers, the boxed-in family pew, with the rows of servants opposite. She thought of the vicar, who must be long dead, and of the nervous young curate, Mr. Baines. Had Miss Grace ever married him? And she thought of Emily. Emily . . . They *had* to see more of her.

Back, in her own time, real and breathing and very much annoyed by her punishment, Emily Cecilia Victoria Roman sat in the schoolroom on a hot Sunday evening and savagely learned French verbs. How could she *help* laughing when that girl Clare nearly fell and brought down a huge cascade of hymnbooks? Of course it was really very wicked to laugh in church. But still the episode had been funny. Especially, of course, since no one had known just why the hymnbooks fell. She was the only one who could see Clare and Richard. They really were ghosts, it seemed, but remarkably solid ghosts, if Clare's arm could dislodge so many books.

She had known, of course, that she would be punished. She had expected to have to walk home again, and she had sat through the Vicar's long, impassioned sermon in sulky gloom. She was hungry and bored, and she and Miss Grace would be late for Sunday lunch if they had to toil uphill, in the wake of the servants.

Oh, *damn* everything! That was how she had felt. And that was very wicked . . . to swear, even in one's mind. Even to know such a word. Emily knew it because she had heard Aunt Ada say it. Aunt Ada said things like that weren't wicked, and there was no hell-fire. It had just been invented long ago to make people behave well.

Aunt Ada had a great many terrible ideas. Well, not

terrible, for if what she said was true, one was let out of a good many things. But even *that* wasn't correct. Emily frowned, as she tried to think clearly, French verbs forgotten. Aunt Ada also said that people should behave well without fear of hellfire. She said human dignity was what mattered, and that everyone should work to try to improve life here and now for the whole of mankind. And especially for women, so that they could be free to develop their personalities and take their proper place in the world.

And Aunt Ada seemed a happy person, in spite of the jeers and disapproval of her brother, Emily's father, and the open scorn of Emily's mother, who was only interested in clothes and entertaining.

"You wouldn't know what to do with the vote, Mary, if you had it," Aunt Ada had said once. Emily had been sitting in one of her favorite places on the window seat in the drawing room, and they had not known she was there. "But you could learn. You weren't born without brains, but you've let them atrophy."

It had all seemed rather shocking until the coming of Clare and Richard Manley. Emily was not sure if they had any reality at all, in present or future, but their talk of improved conditions and the rights of the workers had somehow had an echo of Aunt Ada.

She wished there were someone she could talk to, but there was no one, even if she had not been sent up to the schoolroom and the French verbs. For after the service her mother had said: "Emily, I will speak to you later. You and Miss Grace will return with us in the carriage."

So they had driven home in state, and her punishment had been learning French verbs and going to bed early for three nights.

"I hate everything. I'm bored. I want to go to school," Emily said to herself. "I hope Clare and Richard will come again tomorrow."

The schoolroom was hot and she longed to be free. Oh, how wonderful to be allowed to swim in the lake; to cleave through the cool water, the way she had moved through the sea at Hastings. For she had learned to swim very quickly. At school, girls learned to play games, and they organized secret societies and other amusing things. And here she had no one to play with or talk to, except for Miss Grace, who was dull and obviously thinking of that stupid curate all the time. But Clare and Richard had said she mustn't be unkind.

Clare and Richard . . . *ghosts*. Or else she was going mad. But they did seem real, and everything they said was so interesting.

Emily jumped violently when the door opened and someone came into the schoolroom.

"You poor girl! What are you doing?" asked a lively voice. It was Aunt Ada, looking brisk and rather mannish in a striped blouse and a severe skirt. Totally unexpected.

"I've come to spend the night," Aunt Ada went on. "Not very welcome, but then I never am. How I hate Sundays!"

Emily stared, then relaxed.

"Isn't that wicked? I hate them, too. I'm learning French verbs because I laughed in church."

"Why?"

"Oh, a lot of hymnbooks fell down. I'm so bored. I . . . I would like to do something outrageous. But I did, didn't I? Laughing in church."

Aunt Ada walked to the window. The window looked out over the walled garden to the west of the house.

"I have hopes for you, Emily," she said, laughing herself. "Don't worry, child, for you'll escape from all this one day."

"I don't see how I can," Emily grumbled. "They won't send me to school, and . . . Well, here I am."

"Yes. I know your father seems adamant about school, but he may change his mind. I daren't say too much. He tends to go against the things I say."

Emily nodded, a little embarrassed. It must be awful to be a kind of black sheep in the family, but Aunt Ada seemed to take the whole matter very lightly.

"But even when I'm 'out' and have been presented at Court," Emily went on, still in a grumbly voice, "what can I do except get married? Everyone gets married . . . there's nothing else." Then she blushed and buried her face in her hands, as she leaned against the old, ink-spotted table. How tactless! When Aunt Ada *wasn't*.

Aunt Ada didn't mind, apparently. She said, after a short pause: "Emily, that just isn't true. You *may* get married, but if we could get you properly educated, out of the clutches of that silly governess, or other silly governesses, you could have a career. Women are going to do wonderful things in a decade or two. Some of them do already. But, for one thing, you could start thinking about managing the estate."

Emily gasped, in blank astonishment.

"Me? Father and the estate manager do all that. I—I have no say at all, and never will have."

"Why not? The property isn't entailed; it doesn't have to go to a male heir. It will all be yours one day."

"If—If Father dies. But of course my husband will do it, really. I shall have to make a suitable marriage, and . . ."

Aunt Ada made a rather rude noise.

"Oh, start thinking for yourself, Emily. You're fourteen, not a baby. Develop opinions of your own, and don't just absorb the outdated ideas of your parents. The world is changing. Real, important changes may be far away yet, but *think*."

Emily rose slowly from the table and walked to the window. Aunt Ada watched her approach, leaning sideways on the high sill. The evening light fell across her face, and Emily stared at her wonderingly. Aunt Ada was in her thirties, and she was far from pretty. Yet there was something about her face . . . eyes that were very alive. Aunt Ada never wore frills and flounces like Emily's mother, or most of the other women she knew, yet she was not inelegant. The plain blouse and skirt became her, and her feet were small and well shod.

Emily said hesitatingly: "I—I believe I *have* started to think. Something has happened . . . something very strange. Aunt Ada, do you believe in ghosts?"

She was astonished to hear herself asking the question. Ghosts! Practical Aunt Ada. She would laugh and dismiss all shades.

But Aunt Ada did not laugh. She considered the question and then answered seriously: "We-ell, let us say that I should be amazed if I saw a ghost. I hardly think I'm the type. But . . . Who is really to say? There are so many queer stories. I don't believe in people coming back from the *dead*. But I can believe that time is a very strange thing. That people and events might be going on forever, and the future is there already . . . a logical thread. Why?"

Suddenly, in the hot room lit by the lowering sun, Emily had to speak.

"I seem to have met," she whispered, "a boy and girl from the future. No one else can see them, but my dog knows they are here. And today they were in church, and Clare knocked down dozens of hymnbooks. *That* was real. That was why I laughed. And . . ." She looked at Aunt Ada, who was waiting, and then the whole story poured out. How they had told her she was rude and unkind to Miss Grace . . . how both had talked about workers and their rights, and how, in the future, all the cottages had bathrooms and everyone was prosperous and happy, taking extra money out of the estate in a good year.

"I couldn't have made it up," said Emily defensively. "I couldn't have known that, could I? Even you haven't said that. Though you have said a lot of other things that begin to make sense when I hear them. Clare and Richard have been here three times, and they're so nice. Free, and they wear strange clothes . . . so easy. I was shocked at first. Clare wears *trousers*, and this morning she had stuff on her lips. Paint. But it did suit her. You won't tell anyone? It's really my deepest secret. I don't know why I told you."

Aunt Ada walked around the room, frowning.

"No, you told me in confidence. If I did tell, they'd call the doctor tomorrow, and you are perfectly sane and well, Emily. It must be that Irish grandmother of yours."

"Mother's mother? She died before I was born. I know she was Irish, but I never heard much about her. I don't see what . . ."

"Your mother finds her memory embarrassing, I believe. But she told me about her once, when she was in a more expansive mood than usual. Your mother's maiden name was Mary Dean, but her mother was a member of a very old Irish family, from the wilds of County Mayo. She was a very beautiful girl, but she had strange moments. Apparently the family was mightily relieved when she married a rich English landowner and left Ireland."

Emily was listening intently. "Why was she strange?"

"When she was sixteen, she saw her own father's funeral a week before he was killed in a shooting accident. And there were other occasions when she either saw the future, or glimpsed the past. She had second sight. It seems that a very few people have that gift."

"But you mean . . . *I* could have brought Clare and Richard here?"

"Maybe. I don't know, Emily. But they don't sound as if they will do you any harm. They could even do a lot of good."

Emily said: "The first time they came, I didn't see them. They were very much shocked. They saw Tim Moult being nearly beaten to death in the stable yard. And they also saw Mrs. Brewer, the cook, being unkind to Jenny Moult, the new kitchen maid. Aunt Ada, I never thought before that it mattered . . . that they were *people*."

"If you've learned that, you've come a long way." Aunt Ada remarked. "But I still think school would be a fine idea. Don't worry, Emily. It will all work out. You're a clever girl, and not nearly so spoiled and silly as I once believed. Your parents mean well, and they love you. You must love them back, but you don't have to reflect them. *You* are a person, too. Now I must go. They'll wonder where I am. I'll be leaving early in the morning for a meeting in Bristol."

She had scarcely departed before Miss Grace came in, closely followed by Lizzie with a glass of milk and a plate of sandwiches.

"Have you learned your French verbs, Emily?" Miss Grace asked.

"Nearly," said Emily.

"Then eat your supper quickly and go to bed. Her Ladyship gave me orders that you are to go early for three nights."

"It's too hot to go to bed," Emily grumbled, staring at Miss Grace balefully. Miss Grace had been to church again, and she looked unusually flushed and animated. That curate again! Deep in her mind Emily wondered at the mutual attractions people experienced. Miss Grace seemed to have forgotten all about Mr. Baines' mad father and brother. Perhaps she had asked him, and he had said the story was a wicked lie. In a way Emily hoped it was. She had a dim idea that you might have little mad children if there was bad blood. She didn't like Miss Grace much, but that seemed an awful fate.

"All the same your mother must be obeyed," said Miss Grace.

Emily looked out into the summer evening and was conscious of a wild, pagan desire to run alone to the woods; to fling herself down in bracken or dance in a glade.

"Without all these dreadful clothes," she thought, and knew that she had been wicked again. What would Aunt Ada say to *that?*

But when she had finished her very dull supper, she went meekly to her bedroom, which, like the school-room, looked out on the walled garden.

Tomorrow Clare and Richard might come again. She had plenty to think about at least as she took off her very hot, uncomfortable clothes. It was clear that Clare didn't wear all these frilled petticoats and bodices and long, tight knickers. She had clearly—Emily almost blushed at the memory—worn *nothing* under her cotton blouse. As for horrible thick stockings (Emily tossed them with loathing into a far corner of the room), Clare's feet were bare inside her simple shoes.

Emily donned her long, frilled nightgown and washed her face in the rose-patterned basin. She had taken her bath the night before. How splendid if one could im-merse oneself *every* night, especially when it was so hot. Maybe, in those cottages of the future, people did.

From far below, when she opened her door and peeped out, came the sound of piano music. Her mother was playing in the drawing room. It was a song of the recent war, "Good-bye, Dolly Gray." A sad song, and Emily liked it, but she was sure Aunt Ada wouldn't be enjoying the recital. Aunt Ada knew all about *real* music, and even Emily knew that her mother played badly.

Life was strange, and certainly a little sad, but so very interesting. Manage the estate! What an idea.

"But *could* I?" Emily asked herself, as she climbed into her big and heavily flounced bed. A few days ago she would have thought it one of Aunt Ada's bizarre and shocking ideas, but now she felt more alive, more aware of herself, and her mind was racing with new desires and plans.

It was *hot* . . . far too hot to lie in bed. Emily got up again, pushed her feet into slippers (this was necessary because the old oak floors were worn in places and full of splinters) and softly opened her bedroom door again. The music had stopped, and there wasn't a sound. The schoolroom door was closed. Miss Grace was probably eating her supper in there, or she might have taken her tray to her own room. Bother Miss Grace!

The ancient house was a mass of narrow corridors, with uneven floor levels, and, though it was not yet dark outside, everywhere it was very dim. Emily hesitated, wondering if she should go back for a candle, but, when she turned a corner, a mullioned window gave some light. In another two minutes she had crept to the narrow, winding back stairway that went down to the servants' sitting room and the kitchen quarters. Far below she heard laughter and a deep male voice. That was Mr. Crown, the butler.

Emily went up, not down. Up here were the servants' bedrooms, but none of them would be coming to bed yet. It was a part of the house she hardly knew, and she almost stumbled and fell on the stairs, worn into hollows by countless generations of feet. It was hotter than ever up there, for the sun had been beating on the roof all day. There was a musty smell, and when she looked through an open door she saw a bare, dreary bedroom. There were three truckle beds and clothes littered around.

Emily shuddered, but curiosity and restlessness kept her there. This was how the servants lived, while she had a pretty bedroom all to herself. A rat scuttled away, and there were mouse droppings on the floor at her feet. And then she heard a stifled sobbing.

It came from around a corner, and Emily crept that way. She could not have said why she didn't turn and flee back to the comfortable, civilized part of the house. It was very dark, but she found two steps going up, then looked into a room in one of the gables. A dreary attic room, as hot as an oven, and with three beds crowded into it. There was very little other furniture, only a wooden chair and a washstand with a chipped bowl and jug.

The door was open about twelve inches, and she could see to the far corner. Some light came through the small window, and it showed a small, huddled figure on the most distant bed. The figure's shoulders were heaving, the face buried in the one pillow.

"Why are you crying?" asked Emily, and Jenny Moult sat upright in one startled movement. Her hair was tangled, her face red and blotchy, and her night-dress was very old and far too small.

"*Miss Emily!*" panted Jenny, staring as if Emily came from another world.

"As I do," thought Emily. "Just as if I were a ghost, like Clare and Richard."

Aloud she said: "*Why* are you crying, Jenny? Are you too hot? I couldn't settle down to sleep, either. They sent me to bed early because I laughed in church." She spoke as if Jenny were just another girl, not a despised child from a squalid cottage down in the valley.

"I'm scared, Miss Emily, and I . . . I miss me mother. Cook sends me to bed afore the others, Lizzie and Ellen, 'cause I 'ave to get up first. Being as how I'm the newest and youngest I gets the worst jobs. An' I'm scared of the rats, an' I 'ates being all alone up 'ere in this place every-one says is '*aunted*. An' for a second I thought *you* was a ghost."

"I'm sorry I frightened you, Jenny." Emily wandered around, noticing that there were patches of damp on the ceiling. In wet weather, or in winter, the room would be even more horrible than it was in a heat wave. A few days ago she would have thought it a suitable enough place for the lower servants; now it shocked her. And it *was* eerie up there under the roof, with the shadows gathering more thickly every moment. Jenny was younger than she was, and the cottage she came from might be squalid, but it wasn't lonely.

"Don't cry anymore," she said briskly. "I expect

Lizzie and Ellen will soon be up. And you know, you won't always be the youngest and newest. You might even be cook one day."

Jenny sniffed and laughed.

"Me, Miss? Why, I let the porridge burn yesterday. Cook hit me real hard for that."

"She's a beast, but don't tell her I said so. Don't tell anyone I came. It's to be our secret. I may come again, one evening, so don't be scared. And you think about what you're going to be. *I'll* make you cook one day. You learn all you can. Or you could even be house-keeper. Mrs. Moss won't be here forever."

"Yes, Miss Emily. No, Miss Emily." Jenny's eyes were wide in the gloom.

"So go to sleep, and I shall, too. Good night."

It was very dark going back, and Emily stumbled several times. But when she reached the corridor near her bedroom, someone had lit the lamps. There were footsteps coming up the main stairs, and Emily tried to run, but stumbled again over her long nightgown.

"Emily!" cried Aunt Ada's voice. "I was coming to see if you were asleep. Where have you been?"

"I've been talking to Jenny Moult in her bedroom. Up in the attic," said Emily. "I haven't been there for years, Aunt Ada. It's awful, and Jenny was crying." And then she added passionately: "I see I have a lot to learn. You and Clare and Richard have made me start to think."

"Good girl." said Aunt Ada. "But go to bed now or your mother will catch you. She's coming up to say good night."

10

VICTORIA

On Monday morning the Soames boy and girl came to invite Clare and Richard to midday dinner at North Farm. They were called Jimmy and May and were roughly the same age as the Manleys.

Clare and Richard strove to hide their disappointment, for their only desire was to return to the Manor. But it was clear that they must accept the invitation, for their mother was so obviously delighted.

"Thank you. We'll be there by twelve," Clare told the two Soameses. When they had gone, she murmured to Richard: "It hardly gives us time to go before that."

"Maybe we can go afterward," her brother murmured. back.

They helped in the house, then went to the village to do a little shopping at the store and to leave the finished film to be developed. The woman behind the counter explained that the film had to be sent away, but, with luck, they might get their pictures by Friday or Saturday.

On the way back, they met Victoria Roman mounted on a chestnut mare, wearing an old sweater and slacks. Seeing her for a second time, they still thought her remarkably like Emily. It was uncanny. Victoria dismounted and walked beside them, the reins hooked over her arm.

"I know you're Clare and Richard Manley," she said. "I saw you yesterday, when you nearly got run over. You must have had a fright."

"Oh, we did," Clare agreed. "It was silly of us."

"And you cried out 'Emily!' I heard you. Why?"

The summer secret had such a hold on them that quick deceit came easily.

"You reminded us of a girl we knew in the North," Richard said quickly. It was a lie, but he saw no way to tell the truth.

Victoria looked at them. Her eyes were remarkably like Emily's, as well as her nose.

"Oh, I see. What are you going to do now?"

"We're going to North Farm when we've taken the shopping home. The Soameses invited us for dinner."

"Oh, well . . . I'm glad you've come to live here. We'll go to the same school, you know."

Clare and Richard stared. This was a surprise.

"We thought you'd go to boarding school," said Clare.

"Not me. I never wanted to. I go to school in Painsden, on the school bus. See you later, then." And she mounted and rode on in the direction of the village.

"She's nice," said Clare. "I never expected she'd want to be friends. But the trouble is that we don't want friends yet. Not while there's the Manor and Emily. If Victoria grows curious, what will we do? We can't possibly tell her that we've met an ancestor of hers."

At that moment an elderly man came toward them on a bicycle. To their surprise, he dismounted and walked over to them. He had ruffled white hair and a pink face that looked annoyed.

"Well, that was a mean trick!" he said. "You two . . . the Manley children, aren't you? Left me to pick up all those hymnbooks!"

Clare and Richard stared, in blank astonishment.

"I'm Bill Masefield, the Verger. I was still in the church yesterday morning when you both came in, tidying up after the service. Didn't see you at first, for I was in the vestry. Then out you went, in a great hurry. Couldn't help slipping, but you might have waited to pick the books up. And me with my rheumatism!"

Clare was so bewildered that she couldn't speak. Had they been physically in the *modern* church . . . the church in modern times? And had they imagined all the rest? Emily giggling . . . all that great congregation?

Richard recovered more quickly.

"We're very sorry, sir," he said politely. "It was dreadful of us. We saw that afterward. We should have picked them up."

The old man seemed mollified. He began to mount his

bicycle again, with slight difficulty.

"That's all right, then," he said. "As long as you're sorry."

"Oh, Rich!" Clare gasped, when he had gone. "How quick you were! But I don't understand. Wasn't it real, then? *Weren't* we back in 1902?"

"I don't understand, either," Richard admitted. "Maybe we were in *both*. Mr. Masefield could see us, but we couldn't see him."

"We have to see Emily as soon as possible. Ask her if we were there."

"We're going to be late getting to the farm. Do hurry!"

"I *did* hurt my arm. That was real."

"Yes. Forget it now."

They went to North Farm and found the meal almost ready. The big old kitchen had been modernized, with an electric stove, a refrigerator and all the rest. But the great oak beams were still in place, and Mr. Soames told them that the farmhouse was three hundred years old.

On meeting him, Clare and Richard were at once reminded of seeing that earlier Mr. Soames driving the pony and trap to church. He was very like the other man, though his whole appearance was more contented. It was some evidence that they *had* been in that other time.

Mr. Soames was in a hurry to get back to work, but as he ate an enormous meal, he had plenty to say about the estate. He not only seemed a happy man; he was clearly devoted to the Roman family.

"They're fine folk . . . the whole lot of them. It was

very different in the old days, as my grandfather used to tell me. They were hated then."

"When they lived at the old Manor?" Richard ventured.

"Aye. You've seen the old place? Didn't take you long to find it."

"We don't go there," said May, who was a plump, placid-looking girl.

"Don't go there? Why not?" asked Clare.

May blushed. "We aren't keen. It's a lostlike place . . . kind of haunted. And there's nothing to do there, is there? We'd sooner ride our bikes or watch television."

And there at the Manor, at that very moment—or, strangely, at a different moment in time—Emily might be anxiously awaiting their arrival.

"Don't know much about the country, do you?" Mr. Soames asked, and Clare and Richard shook their heads.

"We've always lived in town until now," Richard explained.

"Then you'll understand nothing about the feeling people have for the land. It's something that's born in you, I suppose," Mr. Soames said slowly. "And it's a feeling patricularly strong in this valley . . . that's what I think. Most of the families have been here for hundreds of years, and not even the bad old days and the bad Romans could kill it."

"But couldn't we learn . . . to feel it?" Richard asked.

The farmer stared at him thoughtfully.

"When you grow up, boy, you'll go away and get some grand job in town."

"Maybe I won't," Richard said. "I might learn farming." And Clare looked at him in surprise, for he had not said this before.

"*I'm* going to town," May said, giggling.

"Not if I know it, my girl!" said Mr. Soames.

But she probably would . . . she seemed that kind of girl, Clare thought. She imagined staying in the heart of the country forever, and found that she rather liked the idea. Already she had a strong feeling for the valley. To stay there . . . maybe marry and bring up her children there, so that they would belong to Romansgrove. It would be good to feel that there were roots.

Mr. Soames went back to work, and the Manleys politely helped to clear away and wash the dishes before Jimmy and May showed them around the farm. It was after 2:30 before they could get away, and, by great good luck, the Soameses didn't accompany them down the farm lane to the gate. Once they were safely on the road Clare said: "I don't know about you, but I'm game to try the old driveway to the Manor. See if we can get through the tangles and if it will work, going that way. It'd be much quicker from here."

"*I'm* quite willing," said Richard.

They pushed past the fallen gateposts and had a terrible struggle through bracken and brambles for some distance uphill. The pendant was safely in Clare's pocket, and she put her hand on it occasionally, almost willing it to transport them to where they wanted to be.

And, as they fought their way to the top of the ridge, it happened, as it had happened when they emerged from Roman's Grove. In a split second the way was clear, and they were almost level with the turning to the stable yard. By their watches it was after three o'clock, but to Emily it would be one hour earlier.

They advanced boldly, making a detour to look into the kitchen yard. Jenny Moult was unpegging dry clothes and piling them into a huge woven basket. She seemed unhappy, and suddenly the cook, Mrs. Brewer, looked out from the kitchen.

"Come on, girl!" she called roughly. "Don't take all day!"

As she turned away, Jenny put out her tongue.

"I 'ates you." she muttered, just loud enough for the watchers to hear. She gathered up the vast basket in her thin arms and went up the kitchen steps.

"I wish we could talk to Jenny," Clare said, as they turned back to the main drive.

Just as they approached it, they heard heavy footsteps coming up the hill, and the sound of subdued voices. Between the bushes that edged the driveway came a group of men, clearly very hot after the walk from the valley, for they were all mopping their red faces with ragged handkerchiefs. The leader was Mr. Soames from North Farm, the man they had seen driving to church; and the others looked like ordinary farm workers. They wore huge, broken boots, shabby trousers and torn shirts that showed their flesh through in places. They were quite a good-looking crew, but all their faces were worn and weather-beaten, and their expressions were a combination of nervousness and aggression.

"I know it be a mistake," said the oldest man there. He looked around fifty. "Sir Alan'll just be unpleasantlike and tell us that if we don't like our jobs we can get out quick. And where'd we go where it'd be better? Us might even get no work at all . . . there's plenty in that state. We can't let our children starve."

"They're near starving already, and in bad health into the bargain," said Mr. Soames. "Come on, lads. We been planning this, so let's do it."

"Last time did no good, Mr. Soames."

"Last time was nigh a year ago. And that farmhouse of mine isn't fit to keep pigs in."

"Pigs do better than us," said the older man, and there was an angry murmur.

"He be a bad landlord. Not all is bad. An' we should have our rights. There's a union for farm workers these days."

"Just you try joining it!" said Mr. Soames. "You'd be out of your cottage in a week. *He'd* not listen to any union, but I mean to try to have my say."

Clare and Richard fell in behind, and so they saw the men reach the front door and pull the bell rope. The butler appeared, and his face took on a look of stern disapproval when Mr. Soames asked for Sir Alan.

"Sir Alan's busy," he said.

"He ain't too busy to see us," said Mr. Soames. "We'll wait."

The butler, beaten by their united front, motioned to them to enter. Scraping their boots carefully before stepping over the threshold, the six men disappeared.

"Good for them! They're going to fight for their rights," Richard murmured.

"Well, it's brave of them, but I bet it does no good." said Clare. "If we go around on to the terrace, we may hear something. Most of the rooms seem to be on that side, and the windows should be open."

Forgetting Emily, they hurried around the house and were rewarded by seeing, through the open drawing room windows, the men being shown into the room. They stood around awkwardly, looking very out of place in the overornate scene. And then Sir Alan Roman entered the room. His face was "black with fury," as Clare said later, and he immediately started berating the men, saying they ought to be at work and not wasting his time.

Mr. Soames, with stolid persistence, heard him out, then said: "We'll make up for it later, Sir Alan. Meanwhile, we want our say. All the cottages are in a disgraceful state. The last thunderstorm proved there isn't a sound roof in the place. And North Farm isn't fit to live in. Added to that, there are doubts about the water supply in the village. Bad throats, people have, and stomach trouble. Next it'll be scarlet fever or diphtheria. Something must be done. The water should be tested . . ."

"The water's as good as it ever was," Sir Alan Roman said impatiently. "As for the cottages and North Farm . . . do you think I'm going to spend a fortune on them? What was good enough for your fathers is good enough for you. So get back to your work and be thankful you have work to do, and money coming in. I could dismiss the lot of you, turn you out of your homes, tomorrow. Plenty would be glad of your jobs."

"Things have changed since our fathers' day," said Mr. Soames doggedly. "People think different. And the houses are just that much older. How long's it going on, that's what I want to know? Here are you, living in luxury, your daughter petted and spoiled. While my children sleep in damp beds every time it rains, and the children in the village are sickly and . . ."

Clare jumped violently when a voice said in her ear: "It's no good, you know. Papa won't listen to them or spend a penny on the houses until they fall down. It's awful, but it is true. Come and talk to me. Come and see the walled garden. I'm so glad you've come."

It was Emily, keeping carefully out of sight of the window. She was wearing a blue dress and was holding her dog firmly under her arm.

"It's terrible!" Richard said, as they followed Emily along the terrace. "Your father must be a monster."

"Well, he isn't very popular," Emily said, over her shoulder. "Aunt Ada once told him they'd lynch him some day. I thought that was very shocking and unlikely when I heard her say it, but now I've started to think and I feel the houses should be repaired."

She hurried around the corner, opened a gate and led the way into a charming walled garden, where beds of summer flowers were edged with low box hedges. The smell of box was strong in the hot sunshine.

Facing them, Emily went on: "Now we can talk. Let's go over into the far corner by the peach trees. Look! That's the schoolroom window, and next to it is the window of my bedroom."

"Couldn't we go inside and see?" Clare asked.

Emily hesitated, and Clare laughed. "They couldn't see us."

"No, but it would be awkward just now. Miss Grace is sitting in the schoolroom. But well away from the window, so she can't see us. Me, I mean."

The schoolroom window was open, so Clare warned: "She may hear you talking to yourself."

Emily giggled, then clapped her hand over her mouth. When she spoke again, it was in a whisper. "You must come another day, and I will take you over the house. You see, I've accepted you. I told Aunt Ada I had met two ghosts, and she said it was my Irish grandmother, who had the second sight. She wasn't shocked or disbelieving at all, and she'll keep the secret."

"Your Irish grandmother?"

"Yes. For one thing she saw her father's funeral before he was actually dead. He was shot a week later."

Involuntarily Clare put her hand on the pendant in her pocket . . . the pendant *and* the fact that Emily might have inherited second sight.

"We took some photographs," she said. "Of modern Romansgrove. The way we know it, I mean. The woman in the village store said they might be back by Friday. We'll show you."

They had reached a sun-warmed corner, where goldenrod and phlox were massed in a big bed. They were just coming into flower. On the high old wall peaches were ripening.

"You think that would be proof?" Emily's eyes laughed at them from under her big hat. "But I would like to see for myself. If you can come here, perhaps I can go *there*. I thought of that in the middle of the night."

"We had that idea, too," Richard confessed. "But we don't know how it can be managed. Did you get into trouble for laughing in church?"

"Yes, I did. Mother was so angry, and I had to learn French verbs. It was very dull, and this morning was dull also. I hate doing lessons in summer . . . it isn't fair. And Miss Grace is cross with me, and only thinks of that stupid curate. I suppose she *must* be in love, but it seems silly to me. Clare . . ." Then she jumped violently when a voice said behind them:

"Emily, why are you talking to yourself? What's the matter, child?"

It was Lady Roman, holding a parasol over her head to keep off the sun.

"I—I was saying poetry aloud, Mama," Emily said, with commendable presence of mind.

"It didn't sound like poetry. Come indoors at once. Miss Blane has arrived to do some sewing, and I wish her to measure you for a new set of underclothes. You've grown so much."

"Can't I come in a few minutes, Mama?"

"No, come now and don't argue, Emily."

Emily pulled a face and was severely reprimanded, then she began to walk away beside her mother. Clare said after her retreating back: "We'll come again to-morrow. Cheer up!"

Emily's shoulder blades twitched under the blue dress, but she did not look around. Clare and Richard watched the two figures walking the neat paths between the tiny box hedges, and both were suddenly filled with a strange wonder that was touched with fear. In the golden luminosity of the summer garden, Emily and her mother appeared not quite solid; there was something slightly wavering about their outlines. Yet the house, mellow and ancient, looked wholly real.

"How very peculiar it is, Rich!" Clare murmured. "When they were near us they were . . . they seemed entirely flesh and blood, but now I'm not so sure." She put out her hand and touched her brother's bare arm. The warm flesh met her fingers reassuringly.

"*We* are real," she said, after a moment. "And oh! They seem so real, too. Do you know, Rich, I dream about them every night. Then I want to wake up quickly because suddenly they . . . everything has all gone."

"I dream, too," Richard confessed. "And they *are* gone, Clare."

"But gone where? Where do you go when you're dead? Or do you just finish?"

"You don't finish in *time*, anyway," her brother said thoughtfully. "That's it, isn't it? It must be. This is all still going on, and that's how we've found it and met Emily."

"I don't like Lady Roman a bit, do you? She's so stiff, and I bet she never laughs. But Emily . . ."

"Emily's quite a girl," said Richard. "She *is* learning to think, and I'm sure she could be fun."

"Yes, we must see more of her quickly. I have the feeling," Clare said slowly, "that this thing won't last forever, and then my dreams will really come true. Some day it won't happen again, and that makes me sad. Time is passing . . ."

"But in a way it isn't. Time is still here; it must be, if

you know what I mean."

"In a kind of way you have a better grasp of it than I have," Clare admitted. "But I'm sure we won't always know the way back. I do love this garden! It smells so delicious. Let's go through that green door in the wall."

The door was closed, and they realized as they approached it that they had not so far tried to open any door or gate. Maybe, said Clare's expressive eyes, they could walk through it. But the door seemed solid, and Richard put his hand on the latch. It swung open, and they went through into a small orchard, where apples, plums and pears were ripening on well-kept trees.

An old man, who was scything grass not far from the door, looked up as they entered, and for a moment they thought he had seen them. They moved aside as he approached the door, looked through the opening in a puzzled way, then closed it again.

"Bain't no wind." he muttered.

In a sudden spirit of mischief, Richard quietly opened the door again, and the man, just starting back to work, gaped . . . his mouth wide open, showing yellowing, uncared-for teeth. Clare seized her brother's hand and drew him away.

"That was mean! Why did you do it? He'll think the place is haunted."

"So it is," said Richard. "By us. I thought it was time we weren't quite so serious. Shall I close it again, then?"

"Of *course* not." Then she saw that he was teasing her and was glad. The incident had dispelled some of the sudden sadness she had felt in the garden, and even the memory of the unpleasant scene in the drawing room seemed less sharp.

They found a well-stocked kitchen garden, where a young girl was picking fine fat peas and dropping them into an old basket. As they stood watching, close to tall rows of green beans, there was a rustle and a small figure approached the girl. It was Tim Moult, looking furtive.

"Lizzie! Give us a few peas."

"An' what'll Mrs. Brewer say?" she retorted. "You ain't no business here, Tim. Is your back better?" As she spoke, she slipped several pods into his hand, and he picked out the raw peas and chewed them hungrily.

"Gettin' better. But I 'ates all them men in the stable yard."

"I 'ates Mrs. Brewer, and so does Jenny. But now Jenny's come, Ellen and I 'ave a better time. Jen takes most of the knocks. It's a nice change."

"Jen oughtn't, then. You should try an' protect her," the young boy said fiercely.

"What, against that great fat woman? Jenny'll learn, like we all 'ave to do. Here, take these peas and run away. If I don't get back, there'll be more trouble." And she rushed away with her full basket, leaving Tim chewing peas. After a few moments, he sighed, and, shoulders hunched, turned in the direction of the stable yard.

Clare went forward and put out her hand to the growing peas. A large, plump pod came away easily and felt warm and real, but when she put some peas into her mouth, they had no taste and seemed to dissolve. She shivered in spite of the heat of the sun.

"They aren't real," she said. "I thought they were, when I held them. So none of it has . . . has substance."

"An illusion of substance, maybe," said Richard.

"But the hymnbooks had substance. They marked my arm."

"They were still there, in the church in our own time. Maybe not quite the same books, but in the same place." He was trying to work it out.

"And this garden has gone, I suppose. There are no peas growing."

"No peas, I'm sure. We didn't come this way when we were here in our own time and saw the ruined house. There might still be a trace of the walled garden. Maybe the walls and the door are still there."

"It's so difficult to understand," Clare said slowly. She would have been glad to taste the peas.

"We've nearly encircled the house," Richard remarked. "Let's go on."

So they followed Tim, but, avoiding the stable yard gate, went slowly back to the driveway, and so in the direction of Roman's Grove. The temptation to stay and see and hear more was great, but they had been late starting and ought to get home. They didn't speak until they were some way into the wood. Then Clare said: "I do wonder what happened to them all. I suppose Jenny grew up and married one of the farm workers and lived in an insanitary cottage. Or had things improved by the time she was grown up?"

Richard shook his head. "I don't know. Things *did* improve, but we have no idea how soon."

"After the fire, but we don't know when that was."

Then once again they walked in total silence through the wood, turning left where the other path led to the stile. When they reached the stile, they found themselves looking across their own familiar valley, with Romansgrove House on the opposite slope. At some moment they had left that other time behind them. And as they leaned there, their arms resting on the top bar of the stile, a voice cried:

"Hey, you two! Why didn't you speak to me back there in the wood?"

They swung around to see Victoria Roman. She was standing a little way behind them, her face dappled by the sunlight and shadow between the trees.

It was an enormous shock.

II

WHAT HAPPENED
TO EMILY

"Speak to you? I . . . We didn't see you," Clare stammered, still not wholly free of the spell that had held her.

"And there I was sitting right beside the path, down near the far end of the wood." Victoria's eyes searched their faces, and their glances fell before hers. "I suppose you've been to the old Manor. Fascinating, isn't it? Most people won't go, but I don't really mind." She paused, waiting for them to speak, but when they were still silent, she went on: "In fact, when I was little, I used to run away there when I was in trouble or unhappy. Once, when I was eight, I planned to spend a night there. I'd had a bad school report, and Dad was mad at me. But they found out what I meant to do . . . saw me collecting food. So I never managed it."

While she was telling this tale, Clare and Richard took the opportunity to climb the stile. It gave them a chance to compose their faces. Victoria might know the answers to their questions, they both realized, but how could they ask her? She was certainly suspicious already. How awful not to have seen her in the wood! They had been somewhere in the past, and she hadn't even existed for them.

"Wouldn't you have been scared at night?" Clare asked, turning as Victoria followed them over the stile.

"Well, I probably would have been," Victoria admitted. "It *is* an eerie place. But it seemed to draw me."

"Tom Moult said he slept there once," offered Richard.

"Oh, Tom Moult. Tom isn't scared of anything. A ghost could come right up to him, waving its ghostly arms, and he'd just tell it to go away." They were walking down the first field, with Victoria a little behind, since the path wasn't very wide. This was a relief, because she couldn't see their faces.

Clare wished she could somehow get a word with Richard. There were things she longed to ask Victoria. If they started asking questions, though, they would surely give themselves away, and how would Victoria accept their wild tale of other times? She jumped as Richard began tentatively: "The house burned, didn't it? Do you . . . know when?"

"Yes, it burned," Victoria said readily. "But I don't know exactly when. The present Romansgrove House was finished in 1910. The date is over the main door. But I believe the family lived at the Dower House for some years."

"The Dower House?" Richard repeated. His eyes met Clare's briefly. So the fire must have happened within a few years of their meeting with Emily in 1902.

"Oh, haven't you seen the Dower House? It's way up the hill, about a mile past North Farm, up on top of the ridge. But it isn't the Dower House anymore. It's the Romansgrove Home for Old People. Estate workers who are too old to look after themselves, and who haven't any family to do it. They have tiny apartments, and there's a very nice woman in charge. She's the mother of the present headmistress of the village school."

"So," said Richard, trying to make his voice sound very casual, "you really look after everyone now?"

"Oh, of course. They all belong to us, and we belong to them. I think everyone likes the Home. It's a lovely house, and they can be alone, if they want to be. But there's a dining room, and plenty of kind people to look after the really sick ones."

"Better than having soup taken to you in a cottage," Clare said, without thought. They were going rapidly downhill, and climbing stiles and crossing the narrow lane as they went. The sun beat down, and her eyes were dazzled by the hard brilliance of the late afternoon light. "You might get it thrown in your face, like Lady Roman that time."

There was a blank silence behind them. Then Victoria said in a very strange voice: "How did you know about that? It's an old family story."

"Oh!" Clare groped for a safe answer. Here was the last field, cleared now by the combine harvester. Ahead was the gate, the road and South Lodge. "I suppose . . . someone must have told us."

"Maybe my father told the story." Victoria sounded more natural this time. "That was in the bad old days. My ancestors were very bad landlords. They let the rain come through all the cottage roofs, and the kids die of diphtheria, but they took soup. Strange, wasn't it? Difficult to know how their minds worked. My father says it's a wonder they didn't get worse than soup thrown at them. There's your mother looking for you. Your meal must be ready."

They escaped from Victoria with relief and raced upstairs to wash and tidy themselves. When they met outside the bathroom door, Richard whispered: "You were a fool saying that about the soup. Emily told us."

"I *know*. It was a mistake. But Rich, couldn't we explain to Victoria?"

"No, I don't see how we can. It was a dangerous enough situation when she saw us in the wood."

"But wait a minute. Rich!" Clare said urgently. "Victoria saw us near the end of the wood, when I'm sure we were still in Emily's time. So was she there, too . . . in that other time? She *couldn't* have been!"

"No, I'm sure she wasn't," Richard answered. "We didn't see her, remember. It must be like the verger in the church. Further proof that our bodies are more or less still in modern times, whatever we think we are seeing."

"But we do see something, and we must be there in a way. Emily proved that all that happened in the church."

Richard didn't say: "Unless we imagined Emily."

After a moment or two Clare went on: "I'm really sorry about Victoria. I believe she'd like to be friends, and I suppose we daren't while this is going on. We'd give ourselves away. But I have a strange feeling she's important. Do you know, Rich, I think she is our friend for the future."

"What future?" Richard asked.

"When all this is over. It will *have* to be over some time. Victoria is so like Emily. A kind of continuation of her."

"Come on downstairs now!" Richard urged.

By the time the meal was over, and they had heard about their father's day, and explained how they had met Victoria in the wood, the affairs of Emily, Tim, Jenny and Lizzie seemed more remote.

Life had settled down at South Lodge. It wasn't perfect, because the habit of irritability is hard to break, but it was twenty times better than it had been for months in the North. And it was clear that their father could find little to say against the running of the estate and the treatment of the workers.

"Tomorrow," said Clare, later that evening, when she and Richard were wandering along the road near the gates, looking across to Roman's Grove, "we'll go again. And all the tomorrows, as long as it lasts."

"If we go in the morning, Emily will be doing her lessons."

"Yes, poor kid. We could take sandwiches and stay away the whole day," Clare suggested.

"Eat them in another time? They'd be pretty stale."

"Well, it might work. We could try."

They went to the Manor next day, Tuesday, and every day that week. Sometimes they went up the old driveway, and at other times through the wood. The change always came as they emerged from the wood, or at least the apparent change. Clare said it couldn't be just there, actually, as they had not seen Victoria when she was *in* the wood. They kept a watch on the path, and there *was* a point when it seemed clearer than in modern times.

Going up the driveway, the change came at different times. Once they found the way clear as soon as they had left the ruined gateposts, and they looked back to see the closed gates and the neat lodge. On another occasion they were almost at the house before they were clear of brambles and tangles of willow herb and bracken.

The day they took the sandwiches and some cake and apples, with bottles of lemonade, they still had them when they reached the terrace. But Emily was not around, so they went, without seeing anyone, into the walled garden and sat on a seat in full view of the schoolroom window. By their time it was twelve o'clock, and they were hungry, so they began on their picnic.

"It's not like the peas," said Clare, munching. "Everything tastes just fine. I wish we could ask Emily to taste and see what happens."

"I don't know if we'd dare," Richard remarked. "It would be like trying to touch her. Maybe better not."

Five minutes later a head with red ringlets poked out of the casement, and Emily waved excitedly.

"Miss Grace has gone out of the room for a few minutes," she hissed. "Oh, I am so tired of geography and French! What are you doing? Having a picnic lunch? What a funny way to have a picnic. There is always *such* a fuss if we have food outdoors. I wish I could come down, but it's only eleven o'clock. Lizzie will soon be bringing my milk and cake up from the kitchen. Then I have to work some more . . . how shall I bear it? Then lunch, which I have to have with Papa and Mama. Mama is feeling a little worried. I have been heard talking to myself: So she resolves to keep an eye on me, and . . ." Hastily she withdrew her head. Miss Grace or Lizzie must have entered the room.

Richard and Clare passed the time by sitting in the boat (Richard wanted to row, but was dissuaded, since someone might see the craft moving in ghostly fashion on its own), and then by looking at the heavy old books in the library. The french window was open, and the room was empty. After that they retreated to the orchard and each tried to eat an unripe apple, but it was no use . . . the fruit was tasteless and unreal in their mouths.

Clare said: "I don't know why I tried again. It scares me. But *our* food was all right."

Emily found them there and at once told them her news. Her cousin, Alan Roman, was coming to stay for two nights.

"And it's such a bore," she complained. "He is so superior and difficult, always telling me I am only a girl. Oh, he's not a first cousin. Something quite remote. He goes to Eton and is sixteen. And what shall I do with him when I want so much to talk to you? I *hate* Alan, and I hate being a girl. Boys have so much more fun."

"It's better now," Clare told her. "In our time, I mean. Girls are just as important as boys. They think so, anyway. Women aren't quite equal yet; there's never been a woman prime minister, or . . ."

Emily stared in astonishment.

"How could there be?"

"Oh, it will come. We'll be interested to see Alan."

"You won't," Emily retorted coldly. "He isn't a very nice boy, though I admit he's handsome. I think they mean me to marry him one day, but he is the very last person I would consider. You wanted to see the house, so come now. Miss Grace has another headache. She dislikes the hot weather. She went to lie down in her room as soon as she had had lunch. Mama says she is not worth the fifty pounds a year we pay her. Such a lot of money! But I believe she really will marry that curate. The Vicar is retiring sooner than expected, in October. And I heard Papa say he supposes Mr. Baines will be as good a person as anyone to be the new Vicar. Papa likes someone he can give orders to, and he seems not to have heard that the Baines family is tainted."

"You won't tell him?" Richard asked, in alarm.

Emily flicked her long reddish lashes.

"No, for I am not certain it is true."

They followed her into the house. She showed them the main rooms, and led them up a lovely Tudor staircase to the next floor. The chief bedrooms were huge and ornately furnished, the beds with canopies, everything hung with flounces. The bathroom made Clare laugh, it seemed so old-fashioned. The bath was so vast, standing on heavily adorned legs, and the toilet had a big wooden seat. Its pedestal was of blue-and-white china, and the whole stood on an oak platform, with something of the air of a throne. Emily was rather shocked.

"You . . . you shouldn't even notice a water closet. It isn't nice in the presence of a boy." She flicked her lashes in Richard's direction.

"Oh, we don't bother about things like that," said Clare, giggling. "Everyone uses them, after all. In our day we can talk about anything. You should hear what they say on the radio. *Anything* can be discussed. Abortion and the pill, and . . ."

"Shut up!" said Richard. "She doesn't understand." Emily didn't understand, but she was blushing. She was also puzzled. "The radio? What's that?"

"Oh, it's a . . . well, a little box, and you can hear people talking in London and in other countries. On television you can *see* them, too."

"See them? In London. It must be witchcraft. I don't believe you," Emily gasped.

"Well, maybe it is a kind of witchcraft," Richard admitted. "But the scientists can explain it. We have a radio and a television at South Lodge. But we don't watch television much in summer."

"I think you both talk a lot of nonsense," Emily said firmly. "Come and see the family portraits."

Most of the pictures were hung in a long gallery at the top of the stairs. At the far end there was one of Emily herself as a child of two. Beside it was another when she was twelve. In that second portrait, Emily was wearing what was almost certainly the pendant Clare had found in the wood. She gripped her brother's hand very hard, warning him not to say anything. Emily might demand to have it back if she understood. But it was interesting to learn that the pendant really had belonged to Emily. It seemed clear that it was the connection. Though how and why it all worked was impossible to say.

"I like that dangly thing you're wearing in the picture," she said cautiously, conscious that the "dangly thing" was in her pocket at that very moment . . . tarnished by having lain hidden in the wood for many years.

Emily sighed.

"I liked it, too. Papa gave it to me on my twelfth birthday, and I lost it soon after. I was very upset."

"Where did you lose it?" Richard asked.

"I don't know. Maybe in Roman's Grove or somewhere around the lake. Alan was staying here, and we had been for a walk. Everyone searched, but it never was found. Mother said probably one of the servants found it and kept it for its value."

But no servant had found it. It had been in Roman's Grove during all the years. It could do no *good* to give it back to her now, Clare thought, putting her hand on her pocket. Once again the mysteries of time scared and puzzled her. Emily had lost her pendant less than two years earlier, so she believed, but as far as Clare was concerned, it was generations ago.

They saw Emily's bedroom, which fascinated Clare.

She looked at all the old-fashioned clothes and boots and longed to try them on. Some of the dresses were very like the ones girls fancied in modern times. But Emily's underclothes . . . Clare laughed over the array in an open drawer, and Emily blushed again.

"You should not . . . a *boy* shouldn't be in here, even a ghost boy."

"Oh, don't worry. I've been in Clare's room a million times," Richard assured her. "But you must find it frightfully hot in all those clothes."

"I do," Emily confessed gloomily, and her gaze went to Clare's slim figure, so obviously free of bodices and cumbersome petticoats.

Clare and Richard wanted to go up to the very top of the house, but Emily hung back.

"The servants sleep up there in the attic. I dare not go again, for I might be seen. I did go on Sunday evening. It was the first time for years. And it is terrible up there; rats and mice and damp patches, and Jenny Moult was crying because she was in bed alone. Once I would have thought it good enough for servants. Now I'm not so sure. In summer it's hot, and in winter it must be freezing cold."

"No one would see us if *we* went," Richard suggested. "We wouldn't blame you. We know it isn't your fault how the servants live."

But Emily looked unaccountably disturbed. She was frowning and seemed puzzled.

"I don't think you should go," she said slowly. "I don't know why, but I feel . . . it would be dangerous."

They both laughed.

"Dangerous? How? Are the floors rotten?"

"They may be in places," Emily admitted. "But I don't think it's that. I just have a feeling, so please don't go."

They went back to the gallery, and Lady Roman was, by ill luck, in the hall below. She had heard her daughter's voice.

"Talking to yourself again, Emily?" she asked sharply, glancing upward. "What is the matter with you, child? I shall have to ask the doctor to come to see you. I am driving down to Romansgrove. I hear that old Mrs. Page is not well. A bore, but it is my duty to go, no doubt. It's really time we got that old woman into an institution in Painsden."

Emily leaned on the gallery rail.

"Mama, wouldn't that be cruel?"

"Cruel? Just common sense. Those people have no feelings. Fetch your hat and parasol, and you may drive down there with me. Hurry, child, and don't argue."

Very reluctantly, pulling a long face, Emily obeyed her mother.

When Clare and Richard went the next afternoon, Alan Roman was there: a long, lanky, handsome boy, sprawling in the blue boat. Emily was with him, and she looked expressively at Clare and Richard as they walked over the grass toward the lake.

"How can I escape?" her raised eyebrows inquired.

Amused, Richard and Clare sat on the grass at the lake edge, and Emily fidgeted with her book, pushed back her ringlets and in other ways expressed unrest until the boy said: "Oh, Cousin Emily, what ails you? I must say girls are a bore. And this place is a bore. I shall be glad to go on to stay with my friends in Taunton."

"You can't go quickly enough for me," said Emily rudely.

"Such courtesy," he said, with a superior air. "But then I don't expect anything from girls. If only you had brains, it would be something."

"I *have* brains, Alan Roman! said Emily furiously. "And girls are just as good as boys."

Her cousin stared at her in such genuine astonishment that Clare and Richard laughed. He was as surprised as if Emily had hit him.

"I suppose it was you Aunt Ada who told you to say that," he remarked, after a long pause. "Well, if you won't read in peace, let us row. You row very badly. I'll give you a lesson."

"No, thank you. I . . . I want to walk."

"Then I'll walk with you, and tell you about last term at Eton."

Alan Roman was tall for his age and elegantly dressed. His trousers were narrow, his jacket well cut, and a straw "boater" adorned his head. He walked with a slight swagger, and he leaned down toward Emily as he held forth about his doings at school, where apparently he was very important indeed. Emily's frustration was manifest in her shrugging shoulders and in her occasional glances behind. But she could not get free. They walked toward Roman's Grove.

In a sudden burst of ordinary schoolboy mischief, Richard snatched up a loose branch and thrust it under the older boy's feet. Alan stumbled and swore under his breath. "How did that get there?" he demanded. "It wasn't there a moment ago. Just like a girl to laugh."

Emily was the victim of helpless giggles and could not speak. Her cousin said angrily: "We won't go into the wood, after all. Take me to see the walled garden. Are the peaches ripe?"

"Why did you do that?" Clare asked her brother. "Silly fool! Just horseplay."

"I don't like him," Richard confessed. "Stupid idiot . . . thinks he's lord of the world just because he goes to Eton. You know Father says places like Eton should be abolished. They will be one day."

But Clare felt differently about Alan Roman, and she was rather ashamed to admit it to herself. The clear cut features under the red-brown hair were so attractive, and he looked quite intelligent. After all, he couldn't help the way he had been brought up. He probably did feel he was a lord of the world. But it wasn't only that. He looked real, and male. She could see, when he turned, faint beads of perspiration on his upper lip, where there were traces of red-brown hair. It was a most extraordinary feeling.

"I couldn't be physically attracted to a kind of ghost, could I?" she asked herself. "And Emily is older than I am, and she isn't. Of course he's impossible, and I wish we could get Emily alone. But there is *something* about him."

They followed Alan and Emily to the walled garden, but it was clear that Emily was never going to escape from her cousin's company, and eventually it was time to go.

"I never thought we'd have to leave without one private word with her," Richard grumbled.

But it was the same the next day. When they arrived, Emily and Alan were just setting off for a ride, accompanied by a groom. Alan looked splendid in his riding clothes, and Emily wore an elegant dark green habit and a black hat. The groom brought the horses to the front door, and the reluctant Emily was helped into the saddle.

While Alan was speaking to the man, she cast a despairing glance at Clare and Richard.

"He leaves tomorrow," she whispered. "I'm so sorry about yesterday and today. I long for another chance to talk to you. I said I had a headache and did not feel very well, but Mama said it would do me good to ride."

"I had heard about this strange habit of talking to yourself, Cousin Emily," Alan said, turning suddenly. Emily went very pink and said coldly: "Mind your own business, Alan, please. I suppose I may speak to my own horse?"

"If you want to be regarded as a lunatic," her cousin retorted. "Let us be off. At least you ride well. I long for a good gallop." And the three riders went off down the driveway.

"She's riding sidesaddle," said Clare, staring after

them. "It does look rather dignified, but very difficult. Alan looks splendid, doesn't he?"

Richard jeered. "More above himself than ever now he's on horseback. Do you really like the look of him?"

It was Clare's turn to blush.

"He *does* look splendid. But he certainly isn't very nice to poor Emily. I rather hope she doesn't marry him. Didn't marry him, I mean. He would be sure to bully her."

"She could have married him," said Richard. "Don't you see, Roman . . . his name's Roman. That must be the way the name went on."

"Maybe she couldn't get out of it," said Clare.

That day they actually ventured into the kitchen. It was empty except for Jenny, who was dismally peeling pounds of potatoes at a vast stone sink. Every so often she sniffed and passed her sleeve across her eyes, and once wiped her nose in the same way.

The enormous old cooking range fascinated them, used as they were to an electric stove and other modern equipment. The kitchen looked older than all the rest of the house, with its dark oak beams and worn flagstones. Two of the walls were of stone, and there was a corner like a cave.

Once Clare, greatly daring, went up to Jenny and tried to put her hand on one thin, drooping shoulder. But there was nothing there; no flesh, no bone. Only empty air. She shivered and blinked, drawing back, and then Jenny was there again, looking quite solid and with a tear trickling down her pale cheek. Maybe Jenny had sensed something, for she turned, with a puzzled air.

The next day, Friday, Alan Roman had gone, and Emily was free again after lunch. They found her reading a school story on the seat in the walled garden.

She greeted them in delight.

"Oh, wasn't it a nuisance that I was with Alan all the time? I was so pleased to watch him drive away to Painsden. Mama said I should go to see him off, and usually I like to see trains, but I had had more than enough of Master Alan Roman of Eton School." Then she laughed. "Speaking of school . . . I think Mama may make Papa send me to boarding school in September. She says perhaps I am too much alone, and she doesn't think Miss Grace is clever enough to teach me. Wouldn't that be splendid?"

Clare frowned.

"I don't really know what boarding schools were like in your time. I read some old stories once, but they weren't set as long ago as 1902.

Emily frowned in her turn.

"You frighten me when you say things like that. Mother speaks of Ferndean on the South Coast. That's a very famous girls' school. Very modern. The girls play games and win matches, and learn gymnastics. She says I may turn into a hoyden, and that will be a pity, but Lord Painsden's girl goes there. The Painsden family has always ignored us. They live in a real castle and know the royal family."

"And she hopes you'll make friends with the girl and get invited to visit at the castle?" Richard asked, amused and a little shocked. He had never met that kind of snobbery before.

"Something like that," said Emily, dimpling. "But she's older than I am, and I shall make what friends I like. I don't care what *reasons* Mama has, so long as I go to school."

That afternoon they took Emily through the wood, for, though she had said talk of later years frightened her, she was brave enough to want to see things for herself if she could.

"I'm not supposed to go alone," Emily said, as they slipped into the trees. "But I'm not alone, am I? Now tell me, as we go, about Romansgrove. Tell me everything . . . everything you can think of about *your* world. It makes me shiver, as if a goose were walking over my grave; but if there are things I don't know, then maybe I should learn about them. It's only when you say things suddenly, casually, that I am really scared. One side of me *does* accept that you have another world. Though sometimes, when I awake in the night, I still think it is a trick."

Tell her everything? About men (not women) going to the moon and atomic warfare and radar and planes flying all over the world every minute of every day, so that great oceans were crossed in a few hours. They tried, with Emily growing more and more incredulous. And then they came to the stile, where there was a clear view of the whole valley.

For the first time, from that viewpoint, Clare and Richard saw the valley as it used to be, with no great house on the opposite slope, and the farms and the village lying among trees, with no newer houses, no television aerials and no cars passing along the distant road.

It was a bright day, though cooler than it had been. One curious thing was that the weather had never much changed when they went into the other time. Perhaps it had been a little warmer, or more cloudy, but never startlingly different.

They had left South Lodge in the same brilliant sunshine, with high white clouds moving in front of a brisk breeze. The valley was lying in such clear light that every detail stood out. Down in one of the fields below them a great wagon, drawn by two shaggy cart horses, was half-laden with wheat sheaves, and men in ragged shirts were busy completing the load. It was a very different sight from the quick work of the combine harvester, and Clare and Richard stared in deepest interest.

"It's fascinating!" said Clare. "But how hard those men have to work."

"But of course they work hard," Emily said. "They'll work until sundown. I suppose you have a *machine* to do that?"

"Yes, we do. We didn't tell you . . ."

But, as Clare spoke, the scene began to waver before her eyes. She blinked at it and then glanced at Richard, leaning on the stile beside her. Emily was a little behind them. Richard was blinking, too.

"It's dissolving," he said. "How strange!"

"It's gone, and we're back." Clare clutched his arm. "Oh, Rich, it was different that time. Not so quick. Oh, I am so sorry! I didn't want to leave Emily just yet." And then she turned and saw Emily still standing behind them. Her face had the lost, blind look that had been on Richard's the first time they went to the Manor. And Clare said very peremptorily, and as quickly as she had done that first time with Richard:

"Emily, come on! Come with us! *Look!*"

The blind look left Emily's eyes, and they parted to let her lean on the stile.

"What happened? Where am I?" Emily asked.

12

EMILY SEES

"Don't be scared," Richard said. "It's all right. It's wonderful, Emily. You've come with us."

Emily was shaking a little, but she was a girl with courage, and, after a few moments, she pushed back her big hat and focused her eyes on the valley.

"It *is* different," she said. "All those new houses near the village. Are they the ones with bathrooms?"

"Yes, but the old cottages have bathrooms, too. We told you," Clare said.

"And all those tall poles carrying wires . . . and what are those things on the roofs?"

"Television aerials."

"So they can see those little pictures inside their

houses? I don't believe that," said Emily. "Things happening in London." She frowned. "But you told the truth about some things, so maybe that is true also."

Then Emily's gaze traveled to the opposite slope of the valley, and Richard and Clare exchanged glances. This was going to be the hard part; something they dreaded having to explain. If they could get out of telling the whole story, they knew they would be glad.

"That great, ugly house!" cried Emily. "Who has dared to build on *our* land."

"Let's start walking," Clare said quickly. "We'll help you over the stile, Emily."

But Emily laughed at that.

"Thank you, but I need no help. I can climb stiles. Miss Grace says I am a tomboy." And she did climb the stile very neatly and quickly, in spite of her long skirts.

As they started down the field, she returned to the subject of the big house on the opposite hill.

"It is a dreadful house! I want to know who dared to build it in that place?"

"Your own family built it," Richard explained slowly. He wished that he and Clare could have a chance to talk privately. It certainly did not seem the time to tell Emily that her home had burned down; she had had one big shock already.

"And we live in the South Lodge. We'll show you," said Clare.

"You mean . . . my family of the future?" Emily looked strained with the effort of understanding. Both Clare and Richard hoped that her thoughts would not carry her too far. For where was she now, this ghost

girl in her long, pretty dress, walking through the barley field?

"But why would they do that?" Emily asked. "Who lives in the old manor in *your* time?"

Luckily her attention was caught by a new sight. In the next field was the combine harvester, neatly and rapidly doing the work of several men. Emily stopped and stared, entranced. But after a few moments she frowned.

"It's very wonderful, but it means that men must be out of work, surely?"

"I think everyone has work," Richard told her. "They do other jobs, and some look after the farm machinery."

A jet screamed across the sky as they neared the road. Emily flung herself flat on her face in the golden stubble. When it had gone, she slowly raised a white face.

"Oh, what was it? That terrible thing?"

"Just a plane," Richard said. "We told you. It's quite all right, really, Emily. It's gone."

"But people . . . *people* couldn't be up there in that thing?"

"Oh, they are. Probably going to America."

"I shall never understand," said Emily faintly, walking slowly on. "It can't have been such a shock for you, coming to my time. We are quiet and peaceful in 1902."

"Here we are by the road," said Clare. "And do be careful of the traffic." She was using all her imagination to try to understand what the experience must mean to Emily. It was true what she said; *they* had seen some sights that they thought cruel and terrible, but they had found a world that, in a way, was easier to accept.

Emily climbed the stile and walked toward the gates of Romansgrove House. She stood with her hands clasped behind her back, staring at the gateposts.

"But they have moved the Roman heads!"

"Look at our little house," Clare said urgently. "This is where we live, Emily." And, as she spoke, she wondered what would happen if their mother saw them. Most likely she would not be able to see Emily, as Lady Roman had not been able to see them.

"It's very small," Emily said doubtfully. "But I want to know about this big Romansgrove House . . ."

At that moment a car came very quickly along the road. Emily, white-faced again, hurled herself out of the way.

"We do have to be careful of the traffic," said Richard. "Come on, Emily. Don't you want to see the village as it is now? We don't know how long this will last, do we?"

Emily had retreated against a high bank.

"Was that a car? I have seen motorcars in London, but nothing like that. How dangerous it must be. Dangerous to be in such a vehicle, and dangerous on the roads, too. Yes, I do want to see the village, but I'm scared. I don't want to stay here forever. What if I can never go back?"

"You'll go back," Clare said gently. "*We* were very scared at first, you know. But it happens quickly. Oh, Emily, do enjoy it. It really is a wonderful adventure."

They walked on, with Clare and Richard making sure that Emily kept close to the hedge. They came to the new houses and the estate office, and they explained about their father. Tom Moult suddenly walked toward them, with his dog at his heels. It was a bad moment, but Tom could not see Emily . . . that was obvious.

"Hello." he said casually, as he passed them.

"What a nice-looking, healthy boy!" said Emily. "He reminds me of someone."

"Of Tim Moult in your stable yard," said Richard. "This one is *Tom* Moult."

As they passed the last of the new houses, Clare caught the glow of a television set through a window.

"Emily," she said. "You go and look through that window. They won't see you, but you'll see television pictures."

Emily obeyed. They stood watching her back view, and, though she seemed so real near them, there was something wavering now about her outline.

"We *will* have to tell her about the fire," Clare whispered. "But not now. She couldn't take it. Not with everything else."

"I know," Richard whispered back. "Oh, Clare . . ."

Emily turned and joined them again. Her eyes were wide.

"You *did* speak the truth. For I *saw* London. There was a procession. I saw Westminster Abbey on that little thing in there. It's magic!"

She walked almost in silence around the old village. Everywhere were healthy, cheerful children, well dressed and well shod. The cottages seemed to interest her particularly.

"In such good repair," she murmured, as they walked toward the village store. "Papa will never repair the cottages. You know that. Papa doesn't mean to be a wicked man. He just does not understand about people. And a bathroom in each, really? Why, they just have a village pump in . . . in *my* time, and some people say the water is bad. The pump has gone."

"No," said Richard. "We found it three days ago. See those neat bushes at the edge of the green? Well, there's a little path, and the pump is there. There's a notice saying it has been preserved, but the water is unsuitable for drinking."

"Children died of diphtheria," Emily whispered.

They stood together, looking into the window of the store. Clare turned to Emily to point out the big refrigerator standing just within the store, and her heart leaped with surprise and shock. For it was not Emily standing there near them, but Victoria. Richard turned at the same moment and gave a cry, hastily stifled.

Emily had *gone*. Emily with her red ringlets, big hat and pretty, old-fashioned dress. Emily, with her wonder and fear.

The shock was so enormous that there was no hope of their concealing it, and Victoria's thoughtful eyes swept over them.

"Did I startle you?" she said. "I'm sorry. You looked very absorbed, the pair of you. What's so interesting in the window?"

"Oh, nothing really," Richard managed to say. "We . . . We came to see if our photographs are ready. They weren't this morning, but Mrs. Potts said they might come this afternoon."

"Some have come. I got mine," Victoria answered.

She was still staring at them with eyes that were so like Emily's.

"What's the matter?" she asked. "You both look so strange. Have you been in Roman's Grove again?"

"Ye—es." Clare stumbled. "Let's go and get the pictures, Rich."

They went into the little store, and their pictures were ready. They cost a terrible lot, but their father had given them extra money, in a fit of benevolence.

Victoria was still there when they came out.

"I really have to go," she said. "Mother's expecting me. But I wanted to see what you took."

All the photographs had come out; that was clear from the price. Into both their minds came the thought of the ones they had taken of the Manor whole, and Emily, Miss Grace and the servants walking down the old driveway. But Victoria so clearly meant to see them that Richard slipped the color prints from the yellow envelope. The ones of the village had come out splendidly. As he went on, looking at each and passing them to Clare, his face changed. Silently he handed over the last few prints. They showed the ruined Manor, sad and deserted, and an overgrown pathway, with the slope of the valley rising on the other side.

"Is that the old driveway?" Victoria asked. "You found it, then? Isn't it tangly?"

"Yes. We . . . we took that picture on Sunday morning." A Sunday morning of bells calling almost a whole population to church. The Roman family being greeted subserviently; a vicar, long dead, settling down to preach a long sermon about hellfire.

Victoria's bicycle was propped up near by. She gave them a last searching look, said good-bye and cycled away in the direction of Romansgrove House.

Hardly knowing what they were doing, Clare and Richard found themselves approaching the lych-gate to the churchyard. Once inside, they sat on an old iron bench under a yew tree and stared at each other.

"Victoria knows something," said Clare.

"I don't see how she can. She only thinks we are behaving in a peculiar way," Richard remarked.

"Well, it's lucky she was in a hurry. Let me look at those pictures again." Clare glanced at each print, then lingered over the last ones. "So perhaps we didn't see it all . . . whole and beautiful," she said sadly. "And the driveway, with everyone walking on it."

"I think *we* saw it," said her brother, frowning. "But the camera didn't. We can show them to Emily, for we *have* to tell her that the house turned into a ruin. I believe she ought to be warned, though we must try not to scare her too much. I wonder what happened to her?"

"I hope she didn't go back to the Manor and *find* it a ruin. What if she's still in modern times?" Clare asked worriedly.

"No, she can't be. I'm sure she went back," Richard said. "Emily disappeared and Victoria was there in her place. We'll go tomorrow, and then we'll find out."

"It seems a long while to wait." Clare rose slowly and began to wander among the old graves. The churchyard was a pleasant one, with shady chestnut trees and great dark yews that looked very ancient. Close to the path that led to the church door the grass had been cut recently and there were some rosebushes in full flower, but the rest of the place was a summer riot of long grass, wild flowers and ferns. It did not seem as if anyone worried very much about caring for the old graves. Many of the headstones and stone tombs were moss covered and half-buried in grass, tall daisies and brambles.

Clare picked her way carefully past a few newer graves and began to peer at the old ones. Richard followed, knowing what she was doing.

"We might find *them*," Clare whispered. "It scares me to think of it, but we ought to know."

"These look very old indeed." Richard scraped away moss and revealed a date: "1795." He went on, saying: "Too early by far. Let's try that corner. And maybe there are memorials in the church. Sure to be, really."

Clare suddenly remembered what she had vaguely noticed on Sunday morning, at the service. "Yes, there are. I saw a window with the Roman arms, and some tablets on the walls . . . all with the name of Roman. But of course that would be too early."

"I saw those, too." Richard was stepping carefully through the long grass, pushing aside flowers and evading brambles, glad to have something concrete to do. "Here's one," he said. "This ornate tomb, with carved helmets and angels. It says 'Sacred to the Memory of Sir Alan Roman of Romansgrove. Died 1909.' And look! On the other side . . . 'Lady Mary Cecilia Roman, widow of Sir Alan Roman, departed this life February 22, 1922.'"

They leaned lightly on the stone, both remembering the arrogant man and the good-looking, imperious, not very appealing woman. It seemed impossible that they had seen her in the walled garden such a short time before.

"1909. So he died before the new house was finished," Clare whispered. "And Emily would have been . . . what? Twenty-one."

"I suppose so. Here's Alan Roman, first Lord Romansgrove of Romansgrove House. He died in April, 1959. That must be Victoria's grandfather. *Clare!* See this . . . this tiny grave with a little headstone. Wait a minute, for it's almost buried in grass, and the letters are very mossy. 'Here lies Clare Victoria Roman, beloved daughter of Emily and Alan Roman of Romansgrove House. Died in infancy, August 23, 1913.'"

A shadow had passed over the sun, and Clare shivered.

"Emily's little daughter! But *Clare* . . . one of the Romans said there was a Clare in the family, but why would Emily call her daughter by my name?"

"A coincidence," Richard suggested. The sun had come out again, but he, too, felt cold. The dappled shadows and soft flowers and grasses of the old churchyard seemed to hold too much strangeness.

"Well, it's a great big one to swallow," Clare said, and her voice quivered. "Oh, Rich, this time thing beats me! Does it mean she really met us, back in 1902? And remembered, and called her girl after me? But we . . . I wasn't born. I couldn't have been there."

"You *have* been there," he pointed out.

"Yes, but from now. What does it mean? Where's

Emily? We have to find her." And she began to poke into the farthest corner. "She did marry Alan Roman, her cousin, apparently, and they had no title. It must have been their son who was created the first Lord Romansgrove."

They searched for a few more minutes, then it was Richard who bent down in a shadowy, moss-grown corner in the angle of two old walls. "Emily . . . I can just see that," he said, his voice muffled as he crouched to try and scrape off moss. It clung more persistently to the stone, perhaps because the corner seemed damp. "There's an *R*," he added. "Yes, Clare, it does say Emily Roman. Died 19-something. If I had a penknife I could scrape it off. All the lettering is just thick with moss."

Clare bent to look, then withdrew, her face very pale.

"We had to find where she was, but oh, Rich! I don't want her to be dead. It's as awful as the Manor being in ruins, up there on the hill."

"Yet in the morning we'll find her at fourteen, and hear about her adventures . . . what she saw," her brother said quickly. He, too, could not come to terms with the thought of Emily Roman gone forever; her bones in this forgotten corner of an old churchyard. "Let's go into the church," he suggested.

The church did not look much different from 1902, except that the ancient box pews were gone, which seemed a pity. There were the hymnbooks still piled up near the door, and Clare kept well away from them. A few memorial tablets and windows had been added, but the whole place was so musty and cold that they did not linger to examine them.

They walked slowly home through the late afternoon, trying silently to come to terms with the mysteries of life and death and the long ribbon of time.

"It *will* be different," Clare said, as they came in sight of South Lodge. "As we said that first day, there'll be winter. It's the leaves, the thickness of the Grove, and all the grasses and flowers . . . kind of a deepness. I wonder if all country is like this . . . except for the Northern moors, I mean. Or if it's just this valley that seems so strange. But the leaves will fall, and there'll be mud and maybe snow, and we'll go to school on dark mornings. A *big* school, like the one in the North, and we'll have to work. So I think this will have to be . . . played out before that, don't you?"

He nodded. It seemed a long, long time since he had been lighthearted and casual, waiting at the bus stop in a dreary city street . . . playing football on Saturday afternoons in winter. During the months since their father's illness he had almost begun to feel old; much more than not quite thirteen. And the strange adventure since they came to Romansgrove had been fascinating, but almost too thought provoking and absorbing. It might be a *relief* to play football again, running in a cold wind.

When they reached home, they made a great effort to seem ordinary, normal. Their mother was so much happier these days that she had grown relaxed and less watchful, though she sometimes gave them puzzled glances. But to her occasional inquiries, they always answered: "We're fine, Mother. Just exploring."

"You're not making friends," she said, that Friday evening. "New friends. Always alone together."

"We will, Mother, when school opens," Clare said quickly. "There's so much to see and learn. We did meet Victoria in the village."

"She seems such a nice girl. Shall we ask her to tea?"

"Maybe next week," Clare said vaguely. "She ought to ask *us* first."

"Lady Romansgrove said you must go soon. They're having some painting and decorating done up at the house . . . quite a big job. She says they're practically living in the kitchen. I expect, when that is over . . ."

By then they would have seen Emily again . . . several times. Provided, of course, that Emily had got back safely into her own time.

But Victoria . . . sometimes Clare felt a little sad and worried about Victoria. She was only on the edge of their lives at the moment. Deliberately, they had kept it that way. Yet she sensed that Victoria could be important to her, and it would be awful if she no longer wished to be friends when the adventure was over. Briefly Clare toyed with the idea of *telling* Victoria, even though Richard didn't approve. She had a sensitive face, and there was a chance that she would understand. It might be better than alienating her forever. They would need her very much in the future; the winter future of school and ordinary living. Yet in the end it did seem better to wait.

As darkness fell, Clare looked up at Roman's Grove. An owl was hooting eerily, far away in the heavy old trees. She tried to think of young Emily in the schoolroom that looked out on the sweet-smelling walled garden, but the memory of that overgrown grave in the churchyard intruded. "Everything passes," Clare thought. "And yet maybe not . . . because she *is* there still, and we will find her in the morning."

They set out for the Manor on Saturday morning, after a night filled with dreams. Their mother had gone into Painsden, and their father was working. He said he found the estate office peaceful, and there were still things he had to get in order. But he would be home for lunch, and had said maybe they would go somewhere in the afternoon.

They went through the Grove and not up the old driveway, though it was quicker. They were scared of meeting the Soames children if they went anywhere near North Farm. But the path through the wood was now fairly clear, with their comings and goings, and unexpectedly soon they emerged from the trees and saw the Manor whole and sunlit before them. They both sighed with infinite relief and joy when they saw Emily.

"She did get back!" cried Clare.

They saw her as they were walking toward the lake. She was on the lowest terrace, with her dog. The dog had ceased to bark at them, but he ran forward in a friendly way, wagging his tail. They didn't, of course, know if he could see them, but he knew they were there. Emily called him, throwing an anxious glance over her shoulder. If anyone saw the dog greeting nothing, there would be questions. She was always quick to see the implications of her friendship with two ghosts.

She walked toward them with careful casualness, though her face was eager, excited. Seeing her so close, so alive, the grave in the churchyard seemed unimportant.

"Oh, I'm so glad!" she cried. "I could hardly sleep last night because I so wanted to talk to you. I couldn't stop thinking of all that I saw in your time. I have *so* many questions to ask you. When I was there, I was afraid that I would never get back, but I would have liked to stay a little longer. But poof! in a moment you and Richard had gone, while we were looking through the window of the village shop."

"Yes," agreed Clare. "We had quite a shock. *We* were back in our own time, and I suppose you . . . What happened?"

Emily giggled.

"It was strange. Suddenly I was in the old village again, all by myself, which I have never been before, and it is quite forbidden. And the housekeeper, Mrs. Moss, had driven down in the trap to do some ordering. She was shocked to see me there. She brought me home, and Mama was furious; so was Papa. I was sent to bed, and I only had bread and water for supper. But it was worth it. Only, when I think of it, I don't understand."

"We don't understand, either," admitted Richard. How could they speak to her of the luminous shadows of the old churchyard, and of the years that had passed, let alone try to explain something that was utterly mysterious to them?

Standing there in her long dress and big hat, it was

hard to imagine her married, giving birth to a daughter. Hard to believe that that tiny grave in the churchyard really existed, with its implication of loss and pain.

"Emily," Richard went on. "We have some photographs to show you. Where are they, Clare? Oh, they're still real. I half thought . . . Well, then we want to try to tell you *something* . . ."

But, from behind them, an imperious voice called: "Emily, come here at once. Miss Grace is waiting for you in the schoolroom. You are to do some extra lessons as a punishment for what you did yesterday."

And there was Lady Roman. Not dead, but alive and demanding to be obeyed. Sulkily, slowly, Emily was forced to go back to the house.

It was very frustrating. They hung around, hoping that something might happen, but nothing did. The stable yard was deserted, though they could hear someone whistling in the harness room, and only Mrs. Brewer was in the kitchen, sleeves rolled up, big red hands making pastry. Richard, trying to lighten the atmosphere, suggested playing a few tricks on her, just to pay her back for her treatment of Jenny Moult, but, unaccountably, Clare wanted to get away. She did not like the Manor that morning; she could not have explained her feelings at all. There seemed to be a sense of menace there, and of urgency. They had to get back to their own time.

13

THE SIGNIFICANCE OF AUGUST 10

The feeling grew, and, with it, the knowledge that there was something she had to do in Romansgrove village.

"We're not going straight home. We have to go through the village," Clare told Richard.

He stared at her, startled by her expression. "Why?"

"I don't know, but we have to go that way. Hurry, Rich!"

"It's only 11:30. We reached the Manor early."

"I know, but let's hurry now."

So they walked the full length of the Grove and came out on the edge of the ridge, by the path down to South Farm. Clare galloped ahead, climbing stiles fast. It had grown very warm, and there was no wind; the valley shimmered in the heat haze. Beads of perspiration gleamed on Richard's nose as he followed his sister. He was puzzled and a little scared.

"Clare, don't go so fast! Why?"

She didn't even answer. They were in the lane, passing the entrance to South Farm, and around the next corner was the village. Since it was a Saturday morning in high summer, there were a few tourists, their cars parked around the green. Otherwise the village was serene; ducks swimming peacefully on the little pond, a few small children rolling happily on the grass.

On one of the seats near the duck pond sat a very old woman. She was neatly dressed in dark blue and was hatless. Her thin white hair was tidily arranged, and her face was healthily pink. But it was clear that she was very old . . . eighty, even ninety, Clare thought vaguely, as she headed straight for the seat.

Richard, still puzzled, followed. There were occasions when he knew that he was only on the edge of this extraordinary adventure. He had no idea what was motivating Clare now.

Clare sat down on the seat, and Richard sat on her right, away from the old woman. The old woman, ancient hands clasped on a strong stick, turned to smile. She had a nice face, with very bright eyes sunk into lined flesh.

"Good morning," she said. "Seen you before, I have, walking around the village. You're the children of the new chap in the estate office."

"That's right," said Clare. "We're Clare and Richard

Manley. Do you live in the village?"

The old woman waved her hand at one of the attractive cottages across the green. "Oh, aye. Live with me great-niece and her husband. Lady Romansgrove said would I like to move up to the Dower House, but I like to watch the world go by, and young Jenny and Fred say I'm no trouble."

"Jenny?" Clare whispered.

The old woman nodded cheerfully.

"Oh, aye. Plenty of girls called Jenny in my family. I was the first of them. Jenny Moult's my name."

Richard jumped, and the sunlit green swam before Clare's eyes. *Jenny Moult* . . . the little girl in the kitchen at the Manor? Jenny Moult grown very old, but aware and apparently quite happy; not beaten by that early bullying, that early hardship.

Clare asked slowly: "Did you work at Romansgrove Manor?"

The old woman chuckled and laid a brown hand on Clare's knee.

"Goodness me, how d'you know that, young lady?" she demanded. "Maybe Miss Victoria told you," she added, when Clare did not answer. "I did work there; went there as kitchen maid at thirteen years old, and how I hated it. That was in the bad old days. Well I remember the cook, Mrs. Brewer, and that awful bedroom I shared with Lizzie and Ellen up in the attic. Rats! How they scuttled around at night. But then we went to the Dower House, and that was much better. An', a few years later, Mrs. Brewer died of a stroke. That gave me a conscience, like, because I'd often wished she'd drop dead. She was a wicked woman, if ever there was one. Lizzie, me cousin, took over as cook. She was young, an' she used to be schoolroom maid, but she was a good cook. Then Lizzie married the chap at South Farm, and *I* was cook up at Romansgrove House until I was seventy years old. They were happy years . . . Eh, things had changed. I had a wonderful life. Young Jenny, though she's not so young now, says I missed things, never being married, but I had a good life, an' . . ."

Clare and Richard had listened to all this with desperate attention. It was like a miracle. Clare interrupted the flow of talk to ask: "You all went to live at the Dower House? Miss Moult, *when?*"

The old woman frowned, then she said: "Well, I may be old, but I never forget me dates. The old Manor burned down on August 10,1902."

"But that's today!" Clare cried. "It's August 10. Miss Moult, today is the anniversary of the day the Manor burned." She was very white, for they had never imagined that the fire had been so soon. Today . . . that day . . .

"So it is!" cried Jenny Moult. "All them years ago."

"But . . . What happened?"

"Well, it was in the evening, around eleven o'clock. We was all in bed . . ."

"How are you, Jenny?" asked a voice, and a big woman, carrying a laden shopping basket, stood before them. "I been meaning to call and see how you were keeping, but then my Bill had rheumatism, and . . ."

Jenny Moult rose slowly, both hands on her stick. She had clearly forgotten the young people in the interest of seeing an old friend.

Clare and Richard rose also and moved away.

"It was *tonight!*" said Clare.

When they had gone as far as the far side of the green, Richard asked: "Clare, how did you know to go and speak to her? How did you *know?*"

Clare scraped the dusty road with her right toe. She looked scared, bewildered, and she hesitated for several moments before she answered: "I haven't the least idea, Rich. I just felt all wrong at the Manor today, as if there was something else I had to do. Then I realized it was urgent to get to the village. And *she* was sitting there. I suppose it may have been a coincidence, yet something seemed to lead me to that seat."

"I'm sure it wasn't a coincidence." Once again Richard felt that this thing was big, too big, and that he didn't really understand any of it. "And now we know that the fire was tonight. That is tonight back in 1902."

"We ought to ask Jenny Moult more about it." Clare started back across the green, but Richard put out his hand and detained her.

"We can't! Don't be a fool, Clare. Do you want the whole village to know we're up to something? She's deep in conversation with that woman. She already thought it a little strange that we knew about her and were so interested. She isn't stupid, even if she *is* about a hundred."

"She won't be a hundred," Clare pointed out. "Only . . ."

"She's old, anyway, but pretty smart."

"But we have to go and warn Emily and tell her they

must be careful tonight. If her mother hadn't turned up just then, we'd at least have managed to tell her that they moved to Romansgrove House because the Manor burned down. We'd have shown her the picture of the ruined house, and she would have been a little prepared. Now we must not only tell her that it burned, but *when*. We can't just let it happen without warning her."

"But it has already happened, so we're up against the old thing. Can we do anything to stop it? Or even alter events at all?" Richard pushed his hair out of his eyes with a grubby hand and frowned up at Roman's Grove, brooding there on the high ridge.

"We can try," Clare said grimly. "At least if Emily knows it may happen, she won't go to sleep, and she could warn the others. Oh, Rich, that beautiful old house! I don't like the way most of it is furnished . . . all those fussy things in the drawing room and the bedrooms. But it's a really historic house." Then she seemed to realize that she was speaking in a mixture of past and present, and ended sadly: "I wish it could be there still."

"Well, it isn't. It's an overgrown ruin. So you want to go back after lunch?"

"We have to go back!" Clare cried passionately.

They set off along the lane to South Lodge and saw Victoria approaching on her bicycle. She waved some letters and indicated that she had to catch the mail. Clare and Richard were relieved that she did not stop to speak to them, and hurried on all the faster, wanting only to get home, have their midday meal and set off again for the Manor.

But they had forgotten that it was Saturday afternoon

and their father was free. As soon as they had had lunch, he said, they would drive to Chedworth, the most wonderful Roman villa of them all. He didn't seem to notice their expressions of blank dismay, and indeed they lasted only a fleeting moment. But, though Richard tried to talk intelligently of what they were going to see, Mrs. Manley was not deceived.

"Don't you want to go?" she whispered, as Clare and Richard helped her to clear away and wash the dishes after the meal.

"Oh, well, yes, Mother," Clare said. "It sounds a marvelous place, but . . ."

"Your father will be hurt if you don't come with us. What *is* so attractive here that you seem occupied every moment of the time?" She gave them both searching looks.

"It's all attractive, Mother," Richard said hastily. "Remember we aren't used to the country in summer. Of course we'll go with you."

They set off in the car at two o'clock, and the villa at Chedworth was certainly very interesting. Richard would have been totally absorbed if he hadn't kept on remembering that that night—or that other night that seemed so recent—Romansgrove Manor would burn.

"I tell you what we'll do," he whispered to Clare, as they knelt together to look at some tesselated Roman paving. "We'll creep out when everyone has gone to bed and take the big electric lamp and go to the Manor."

Clare shook back her hair and looked at him. Her eyes were brilliant; eager and scared at the same time.

"I was going to say the same. Father and Mother have

been going to bed very early. You know they say the country air makes them sleepy. We could probably get out by 10:00, or not much after, but would we be in time? I know we've got there in less than an hour. But in the dark . . ."

"Don't forget we'll have an hour in hand," Richard pointed out.

"Yes, of course. I often do forget. That should help." And, seeing their father glancing in their direction, she bent to examine part of the design of the ancient paving.

"Aren't you scared?" Richard asked, in a low voice.

"Yes, I'm very scared," Clare confessed. "But nothing would keep me away. I only wish we could go sooner, but if we said we wanted to go up to Roman's Grove after supper . . ."

"Don't try it. They wouldn't let us. We aren't going to be home much before 7:00 at this rate."

They were home twenty minutes before seven, and Mrs. Manley produced a cold supper very quickly. But it was nearly 8:00 before the table was cleared and the dishes washed. Quite useless to suggest that they wanted to go out and stay away until late.

The waiting time was awful. Clare's stomach felt uneasy, and she had a slight headache. The feeling of urgency was ever present, and yet, as Richard strummed his guitar out on the little lawn in the cloudy, warm evening, she tried to think clearly.

"Probably we can't do anything. It *has* happened. It happened long ago. We know the Manor is a ruin and all lost and forsaken. But it really seems to us that Emily is alive and young and living up there beyond the

Grove." She glanced up at the dark, brooding forest, heavy in the late dusk.

"I think we'd better go up the old driveway," Richard murmured between chords. "We've worn quite a path now, and it will be lighter than the wood."

"Someone may see us on the road."

"Have to chance that. It's much quicker from here."

Their parents decided to go to bed when Clare and Richard did. That was at 9:30. Mr. Manley was yawning, and Mrs. Manley said it was funny, but she'd sooner go to bed early and get up early. Quite the opposite from when they'd lived in town.

By ten o'clock the house was silent, and five minutes later Mr. Manley's snores were clearly audible. But they had decided to give their parents thirty minutes in which to settle down. At 10:25 Clare got out of bed again, took off her pajamas and hastily scrambled into her few clothes. Jeans were essential, and the pendant in her blouse pocket was essential, too. The helpful thing was that people in the heart of the country all went to bed early. Farmers had to be up to milk cows, even on a Sunday morning. There was not really much chance of their meeting anyone on the road.

She and Richard met on the landing outside the bathroom door, she holding a flashlight with the bright beam cast downward. The big electric lamp was always kept on a table in the hall. They crept downstairs with their sandals in their hands. Richard took up the lamp and led the way into the kitchen. The key to the little gate in the big one hung on a nail by the back door. The string was in such a wide loop that it slipped easily over his head.

They would be in real trouble if they lost that key.

They opened the back door with scarcely a sound and slipped out into the open air. The evening was very still and seemed, at first, very dark. Roman's Grove loomed, black and secret, across the valley, invisible but for the suggested line of it against the few stars.

Richard locked the gate behind them and they turned right up the road, heading toward North Farm. An owl hooted from Roman's Grove and was answered by one in the trees near Romansgrove House. There were strange little whistling sounds in the air that Richard said might be bats. Neither had ever been out at night in the country before, and it was a strange enough experience, without the thought of what might lie ahead.

But one comfort was that there might not have been a soul in the world. They heard no footsteps on the road and saw no lights. Clare jumped violently when there was a sound behind the hedge, but it was only a cow. Then they heard a car approaching and cowered against the bank as it swished by. After that the world was almost silent again, and the narrow road was very dark between its high, overgrown banks. But they could see a little here and there, with the help of the stars.

Clare walked as if in a dream, knowing somehow that it was inevitable, this heading for Romansgrove Manor in the late evening . . . thinking perhaps she had done it before.

It was ten minutes before eleven as they started up the tangled old driveway.

"It's just as well they are one hour earlier," Richard said.

"Yes, we'll need every minute of the time. I thought you said we'd made a pathway!" Clare gasped. "Oh, Rich, shine the lamp here. I'm caught up in something."

It was a nightmare. In daylight their feet had trampled down some of the growth and brambles, but in the dark it was almost impossible to steer a straight course. Clare held the small flashlight and Richard swung the powerful lamp, trying to help both of them. The night was cloudy and very still, and the few stars were not much help now. Small creatures ran away ahead of them, and the owl still hooted in Roman's Grove above them on the ridge. For the first time both were really afraid of that ancient countryside, yet it was not really fear of its oldness. Just of the darkness, the awful tentacles of the brambles, the waist-deep bracken that tripped them again and again. The very place seemed to be holding them back.

14

A SCREAM
IN THE NIGHT

It was the thought of Emily that drove them so urgently onward and uphill. Of Emily and all those other people perhaps already asleep in the house on the ridge, not knowing that fire was to threaten them in so short a time.

"The countryside is holding us back," Clare thought. "But something else is even stronger."

Richard tripped yet again, and the lamp fell out of his hand, making a brilliant arc of light as it sank into the bracken. Clare retrieved it and helped her brother up. He was panting and so was she.

"What if someone sees our lights?" she gasped. And then she decided it didn't matter really; let people think the old driveway was *haunted*, as in a way it was.

They were nearly at the top of the hill at last, yet the driveway was still the overgrown track of modern times. Completely breathless, they stopped and stared all around, seeing nothing but darkness, here and there just the faint, pale glimmer of a stubble field. And a jet plane suddenly roared overhead, making them jump.

"It isn't going to work," whispered Clare, and put her hand firmly on the pendant.

Richard was still staring back, the way they had come.

"There's a light!" he said softly, suddenly. "Moving. Following us."

Clare spun around again. "There can't be! You imagined it. Oh, no, I saw it then. Below us, on the driveway. Look! It's coming on."

"Father!" Richard whispered.

"If it was Father, he'd have shouted," Clare pointed out. "Oh, come on! There's no time to waste. We have to get there."

They gained the top and suddenly, eerily, they saw the arch of the stable-yard gateway against the cloudy stars. They had missed their way slightly, and they were still in modern times.

Shivering, clutching Richard's arm, Clare turned back, and they headed toward the house. And then, in a split second, all was different. The driveway was whole and clear. And the house was whole, looming high above them. The Tudor chimneys and old gables and dormers were clearly etched against the brilliant night sky, where hung a dazzling full moon.

"Thank goodness!" Clare murmured. "What's the time?"

"Twenty before eleven," said Richard. "*Their* time.

It took us ages to get here."

"But we've done it. What must we do now? Ring the bell? Bang on the door? There's no fire yet."

"Not that we can see," said her brother, and moved on, around the house toward the terrace. The scene burst on them in its dreaming silver beauty . . . the shine of the lake, the long curves of the terraces, Roman's Grove dark beyond.

It was so lovely after the nightmare of the old driveway that they lingered, staring. Then Richard said: "We know where Emily sleeps. Let's try and wake her. Throw gravel at her window."

They went along the top terrace, and Richard glanced at his watch again. It still said twenty before eleven.

"My watch has stopped!" he cried. "Oh, Clare!"

And something was spoiling the serene beauty of the night . . . there was a smell in the air, frightening, acrid.

"It's burning *now!*" Clare shouted, and she rushed to the drawing room windows. The drapes were almost completely across the windows, but there were gaps, and she looked into red-gold light. Great bursting flowers of flame. The fire had started in the drawing room of Romansgrove Manor, and already it had a strong hold.

"Emily!" cried Richard, and they ran, stumbling in their desperate haste. They gained the walled garden and stared up at Emily's window. It was open. In an age when fresh air was not overpopular, Emily had taken a lesson from her Aunt Ada, who preached the benefits of open bedroom windows among her many other strongly held beliefs.

They picked up handfuls of small stones and hurled them upward. In the silence, they heard some of them

fall on the bare oak floor of the room. There had been pretty pink rugs by Emily's bed, but that exposed stretch of floor was a blessing. Surely she would hear the sharp rattle?

Then it occurred to then that they could shout; and shout they did at the tops of their voices, remembering that only Emily would hear them. In any case, it would not have mattered then. And, after a pause that seemed long, there *was* Emily, leaning out of the casement. Her hair seemed to be in curling rags and her nightgown, frills on the neck and sleeves, looked almost silver in the moonlight. She was startled and sleepy, but she called down:

"What is it? What is the matter? I never expected you so late."

"The house is on fire!" Richard shouted. "Wake everyone at once. Hurry, Emily! The drawing room is burning."

Emily gasped, then sniffed. "Yes, I can smell it. And there's smoke coming under my door."

"*Hurry!*"

Emily disappeared. They heard her shouting and banging on a door. "Miss Grace! Wake up! Fire!" And then her voice retreated. "Papa! Mama! Fire!"

Shaken, feeling as if their legs would hardly carry them, Richard and Clare went back to the terrace. The drawing-room windows had shattered in the heat, and the drapes were flaming.

In upper windows faint lights began to show. Candles? Voices . . . shouts . . . more faint lights in the higher windows under the roof. Clare and Richard thought of those awful servant bedrooms up the narrow stairs by the kitchen and apparently extending all over the top of the house. Was there more than one staircase? But they had surely been warned in time? Wouldn't everyone have heard the noise?

The fire was raging, eating into the ancient woodwork of the house. In minutes the room above the drawing room was alight; the ceiling came crashing down in a shower of flame. The long, rose-red fingers of fire licked out across the top terrace, combating the moonlight.

"We have to see! Let's go to the kitchen door; find out if they're coming to safety," Clare wailed. The wonderful moonlit scene had given place to a moonlit nightmare.

"Keep away from the house . . . down to the next terrace!" Richard ordered, and Clare, obeying, tripped on a stone step. She fell headlong, with great force, and the world went dark. Somewhere she heard a peacock screaming . . . or, no, it was a human voice. A dreadful cry of agony and fear.

Then she heard her brother's voice. "Clare! Clare, what happened? Are you hurt?"

"I don't know," she whispered, and slowly opened her eyes. She was lying in a tangle of nettles and bracken, and everywhere was very dark. She could sense, rather than see, the ruined house above her. There was no fire . . . no moon . . . and the Manor had burned long ago.

"I . . . I have lost the pendant," she said, putting her hand to the little pocket where the pendant should have been. "It must have shot out when I f—fell."

And then there was a flashing light and a voice crying "Clare! Richard! What are you doing here? It's Victoria."

The shock of the transition was too great for any kind of caution. As Victoria helped her up, Clare cried: "But it can't be you! It can't all have gone! Emily was here, in the burning house. And we *have* to know if she's safe! What if she *died* in Romansgrove Manor?"

"She didn't," Victoria said, in an odd, breathless voice. "She is asleep right now in Romansgrove House on the other hill."

Clare was on her feet again, and Richard had had the presence of mind to switch on his powerful lamp. The light showed Victoria, so like and so unlike Emily Roman of long ago. Victoria wearing a dark sweater and dark jeans, looking very thin and tall and white of face.

"She c—can't be!" whispered Clare. Her hands throbbed and burned after their contact with the nettles, and her whole body ached after the force of the fall. "Of course, I remember now . . . she had a daughter. She couldn't have died in the fire. But she must be dead, all the same. We looked for her grave in the churchyard, and there is an Emily Roman buried there. You . . . You don't know what you're saying. You don't understand anything!"

"Hush, Clare!" said Richard. "I told you she guessed something."

"I understand quite a lot," Victoria told them. "I know there's an Emily Roman in the churchyard; in that very tangly corner, and you can't read the inscription properly. But that was Emily's aunt; her father's sister. She died unmarried in 1900."

"Her aunt was called Ada," Clare argued.

Victoria gasped. "You do know a lot! Ada was her father's other sister. Oh, don't sound so bewildered. I've followed you up here before, several times. I knew you were . . . were in some other place. I watched you; it was very strange and scary. And this morning I met Jenny Moult on the green, and she asked about you. She was a bit puzzled, and she wanted to know how you knew about her. She told me she had told *you* that tonight was the anniversary of the fire. I had a feeling you'd come, and so I waited near the lodge. I let you get well ahead. Actually, I had to, because I dropped my flashlight and couldn't find it for ages."

"But what about Emily? You can't mean what you said." Richard could hardly believe that Emily Roman was still alive; yet, since Jenny Moult was still living in Romansgrove, Emily could be also.

"Oh, yes, she's alive." Victoria sounded more herself, almost cheerful. "She certainly didn't die in the fire, or any time after. She does have rather bad arthritis, but she's very *much* alive mentally. She's my great-grandmother. She has an apartment in the house, and my grandmother has another. She's Emily's daughter-in-law. I thought you might have learned that from someone. I think your mother knows."

In the mixture of darkness and lamplight, Clare and Richard tried to exchange glances.

"I don't think we have been paying much attention to the present," Richard confessed. "Half the time we probably weren't listening when Father and Mother talked. And we never told them anything about this . . . this thing that has been happening to us. But I mean to," he added firmly. Then: "But no one will ever believe us. They'll think us mad. *You* must. We really did go back, and we really did see people, but Emily was the only one who could see *us* and talk to us."

"I know," said Victoria.

"How *can* you know?" asked Clare.

"She told me," Victoria said, and she sounded as if she were smiling. "We're very close. It has been our secret, hers and mine."

"But you mean she *did* meet us, back then? She told you that?" In the cloudy summer darkness it all seemed more than ever a dream.

"Oh, yes. I believe you did meet. She's extremely sane, and I . . . Well, maybe I'm a little like her. I haven't second sight, or anything like that, but I can understand strange things."

"You're *very* like her to look at," Clare jerked out. "Oh, I'm so glad she's alive, but I still don't understand anything."

"She was in the car that day they met me at the station, and we nearly ran over you," Victoria said rapidly. "When you saw me you cried out 'Emily!', and she cried something, too, and looked rather peculiar. Later she told me she had met two young people just like you, called Clare and Richard Manley, when she was a girl. That was why she called her little dead daughter Clare. She told me about how you went to the Manor several times, and at first she thought you were gypsies, because you were dressed so strangely. She said you woke her on the night of the fire, and maybe saved them all."

"But someone did die," said Clare, shuddering. "I heard a dreadful scream as I fell. I thought for a moment it was the peacock."

Victoria shivered; they saw the faint movement in the lamplight.

"How awful for you! Yes, a girl who worked in the kitchen was killed. Her name was Ellen. She jumped from an attic window."

"The fire has only just happened," Clare said shakily. "I mean, if she remembers us from when she was our age I don't see how she can. It sounds muddled, but we weren't born."

"But you *were* there. It's all too clear to be any kind of mistake. She told me about your coming on the night of the fire days ago, and now you have come, and I saw you looking up at where her bedroom window was. You were standing in what's left of the walled garden, calling up to that ruined window. Oh, don't try to puzzle it out now," Victoria urged. "We must go home to bed. You did other things, too, that affected her. She'll tell you. You talked to her about how awful things were, and how the servants were people with rights. And you talked about Romansgrove now, and how wonderful it was, and once you even took her to see it for herself. So, when she inherited the estate (she did, you know, for it didn't have to go to a male heir), she started all the changes. I think things go in a circle."

"But, if she's alive, it all belongs to her still," said Richard.

"No, after a good many years she made it over to her

son, who felt as she did. He was created the first Lord Romansgrove. Actually, it's a kind of company now: Romansgrove Estate, Ltd."

"Well, if we had anything to do with it because of what we said," Richard said slowly, "it was really Father. We've listened to his views all our lives. Shall we see her? Emily, I mean?"

"Oh, yes. She wants you to come up to the house in a day or two. Just after that car ride her arthritis was especially bad, and she didn't feel like seeing visitors. And then there was all the bother about the decorating. But, of course you must come. She wants to talk to you."

"Talk to Emily!" Clare marveled. "But . . . I would be scared. I suppose she's a tiny, wrinkled, white-haired old woman? *Very* old."

"She's small," Victoria said, "but not very wrinkled. She has a wonderful complexion. And her hair still has some red. She has it touched up a little, but not much. All the people on the estate adore her. And now, do come on!"

Dazed, still longing to ask a thousand questions, they started back to the valley, through the tangle of the old driveway. It was a relief to reach the road and to walk on through the bat-haunted, owl-loud night.

"We're sorry we didn't tell you," Clare said. "In a way we wanted to, but we thought you might think us mad. It's still very hard to understand. We didn't know you were following us. You don't mean . . . that you went back, too? That *you* could see some of it?"

"No," said Victoria, "I never saw it myself. I don't think I have powers like that."

"You said you could tell we were in some other place . . . you mean some other *time*," Richard said slowly. "So it was what we thought? Our bodies were still visible in our own time. It's a good thing we weren't seen by many people. But, Victoria—" his voice took on a note of shock—"we went into the house. Did we do that, really? We went into the library, and the drawing room, and once we went *upstairs*. We couldn't have climbed a staircase that wasn't there anymore. We went into Emily's bedroom, and the bathroom near by, and we wanted to go into the attics, but Emily wouldn't let us. She said . . . it was dangerous. But she didn't seem to know why."

"It would have been dangerous," Victoria said very gravely. "It was after I saw you coming out through the ivy near where the drawing room window used to be that I got really worried. I knew it couldn't go on for much longer. You might have hurt yourselves."

"But . . ."

"Did you ever see the house as it is now? Apart from tonight I mean?" Victoria asked.

"Yes, once. The second time we went. The . . . the spell didn't work. We didn't like it. We were upset," Clare explained. "Rich looked at the stones and said he thought the house had burned. We went away quite quickly into the stable yard, but Rich did say he thought we could get in if we wanted to."

"You can get in," Victoria said slowly. "The ivy has grown over very thickly, but there are several places where you *can* manage it. I've been in the kitchen . . . part of it was all stone and didn't burn. But it's quite open to the sky."

"But the staircase, Victoria!" Clare gasped. They were almost at the gates of Romansgrove House.

"Well, you know that western end of the house is still quite high, though roofless. The wooden staircase burned, of course. Father took me in there once, when I was little. After the house was burned they did, at first, think it should be rebuilt. They even started on the work. I've learned some of this from Great Grandmother during the last few days. Her father soon changed his mind, however, and decided to build on the opposite hill. But *some* work was done. They put in a temporary staircase, so that the men could reach what was left of the upper floors."

Clare and Richard had both stopped and were staring at her in the dim light.

"And we went up that?" Clare whispered.

"You must have. That corner where Emily's bedroom was wasn't much damaged, and they repaired the floors. *But* most of the attics had gone, of course. There *was* danger to you. Though I don't know how Emily knew," Victoria said, rather shakily.

"We might have been found dead in the ruined house." Richard sounded shaky, too.

"But you weren't."

Victoria used her key to open the gate, and they all slipped in, parting with a few whispered words. Clare and Richard crept into the silent house, locked the back door and went to their rooms. They were undetected, but both knew that some day—though maybe not for quite a long time—they would have to tell the strange story.

Clare leaned on her windowsill for a few minutes. The valley slept . . . even the owl cries and the faint squeaking of the bats had stopped. The modern people of Romansgrove slept in the old cottages and the newer houses; the ones of the past slept, too, in the shadowy peace of the churchyard.

In this country, as perhaps in all country districts, there was continuity, a constant belonging.

And Rich and she understood it better than almost anyone else, Clare thought. For they had seen what it was like once, and people who were real then. Tim Moult led straight to Tom, somehow. And it must be true of lots of others. And, of course, there were Emily and Jenny, who weren't dead at all. Who still lived and belonged, and now she and Richard belonged, too. They'd always belong. And surely there'd never be any reason ever to go away.